I0689360

The Nights and Times of Ned Clery

Nancy Guild Bendall

Toronto, Canada

ISBN: 0993904904
ISBN 13: 9780993904905

for Ian …

who is the best of me

Table of Contents

Foreword

Nancy Guild Bendall's *The Nights and Times of Ned Clery* is much more than just another book for children. After finishing it and then scanning it another couple of times I predict that it has the potential to become a treasured volume for all ages. Ostensibly it is aimed at the eight-to-nine-year-old reader, and I tested it on a nine-year-old grandson to see if it was accessible to him. 'It's not hard,' was his summary.

Yet I prefer to think of *Ned Clery* as a book for adults to read *to* children of all ages, for all that it is accessible to literate nine-year-olds. I prefer this not just for the rich oral sense of the author's language, but for the satisfaction that the process of reading this book aloud to children will afford to adults and children alike.

Ned Clery is the central character who experiences a series of adventures made possible by his Rhyll, a mushroom-like creature that mysteriously appears near his father's green house. The 12 adventures are spaced across about five years, so that Ned is 15 by the time they are over: enough reading for a fortnight of bedtimes. The early adventures take him to the strange worlds and dimensions of fairies and such. By the end of the book, he has been to a moon settlement filled with adventurous elements of science fiction.

That it is a prime candidate for those families where time is made for reading aloud and for common reading enjoyment - the kind that includes stopping to think and talk about the story - would be enough to recommend the book as an important addition to the family library. But Guild Bendall offers more - much more.

First, the book is self-illustrated. There are 13 full page illustrations connected intimately to the chapters of the book, each created by the author in a totally modern medium that uses a touch-screen layering process to create luminously evocative images, adding to the magical, 'out-of-this-world' effect of the narrative. I found myself referring back to these illustrations frequently as I read, and I'm sure children would be equally eager to keep them in mind.

Like the narrative, Guild Bendall's art draws from a number of rich traditions, blending them into something of her own. The notion of telling stories in silhouettes or shadows is as old as Chinese Shadow Play, and as modern as the shadow animation of German film animator Lotte Reiniger, whose works date from 1919 to 1979. Guild-Bendall has used her colour images to illustrate not just a single moment in the story but to represent the story-at-once, something that is more like a medieval tapestry or a church window diorama than a traditional book illustration.

Second, Guild Bendall's style is inclusive. She does not speak down to a young audience, but grants them her assumption of a literacy and curiosity well beyond the expectations of reading text books of elementary school; an assumption that I predict will be rewarded with a large audience of both young and older readers. She assumes that her readers, even if they no longer believe in fairies, are open to stories about them.

Third, she is part of the tradition of timeless story-telling. She provides a modern version of many tropes that have long been the stock-in-trade of traditional and fantasy story-telling, always celebrating themes and conventions without trespassing. Some of the early stories have a Lewis Carol sort of feel to them, while one or two of the later ones reveal the author's homage to late nineteenth century science fiction from the likes of H.G. Wells and Jules Verne.

And fourth, she can write. There is none of the controlled-vocabulary or limited syntax nonsense of the supermarket trade in books for young people. There's plenty happening on every page; however, things like pausing to describe the scene, to explore feelings or to ask questions don't strike the reader as interruptions, but as value-added to the story.

The combination of and appeals to so many different styles and conventions of narrative, together with an altogether innovative form of illustration art: these are characteristics of postmodernism, if the theorist in you craves a category.

Guild Bendall's stories are rich and rewarding narratives. Her language takes flight when it feels the need, inviting all readers to fly along for the adventure.

Chris M. Worsnop
Reading curriculum specialist
Media educator
Lover of good books

Chapter One:
Ned Meets The Rhyll

As Ned Clery later recalled, there was a full blue moon in a cloudless sky that night in the month of May, in the tenth year of his life – that night, that exquisite moment, that delicious second when he first introduced himself to the Rhyll. Of course he didn't know at that time that it was a Rhyll – he learned that later. All he knew was that it was strange, mysterious and alien-looking. It only took the briefest of glimpses from a distance to launch his spirit of adventure. He didn't even know that he had a daring bone within him and he didn't even know what that meant yet. But once he saw *what* he saw from his third storey window, there it was – his adventurous spirit.

For what must have been the hundredth time Ned peaked through the greasy window of his stuffy attic bedroom. Of course he should have been asleep in his bed by now, hence the need for stealth. But he had glimpsed something bright green in colour, no more a glowing green ... 'thing' he was going to call it for now, plunked down in the middle of his tiny garden at the far end of his parents' property.

What made him pay particular attention was the fact that it was in his garden patch, his private territory that Dad had allowed him to plant on his own. He took great pride in this new project, all the more so from being a fairly lonely boy living at the edge of a village where almost no children his age lived.

Chapter One

When he gave him the space, Dad had also given him ten dollars to plant this humble bit of earth, just ten dollars to buy seeds. Ned was up to the task. For his very first garden, he chose vegetable seeds. He selected a rainbow of carrots from a seed catalogue – purple, yellow, red and orange. Next he bought two types of beets, both white and red, because he had never eaten white beets and wondered if they would be as delicious as the red ones. For his tomatoes, he picked grape-sized. He found these tomatoes were sweet-tasting, and he liked how they popped in his mouth when he bit down on them. Finally, for Mom, he chose little leaf lettuces, which he planned to plant a few at a time so that they would not ripen all at once, which just might result in the disastrous consequences of him being force-fed a green salad every single day!

He had prepared his garden carefully. Hoeing the ground to loosen the soil as he had seen Dad do, he had then taken all the weeds he could see from the bed. Next he sprinkled some mulch from the compost pile over the top and raked it in until it was smooth and level. He planted his seeds in nice even rows, well-spaced so that they could stretch their leaves out without touching one another. Lightly covering them with soil, he watered and waited. He waited, watched and watered every day with Dad's big watering can. He had even weeded on two occasions, both times on a weekday, just after he came back on the bus from school, and before supper. Now two weeks on, as he watched his seeds begin to grow into young plants, Ned dreamed of the day when he would see them on their dinner table, and in his reveries, he saw Mom all puffy with pride in him, and he would feel special.

Now Ned knew that he wasn't special – knew it for certain. He was half a head shorter than most lads his age. He was certainly scrawny, although Mom would say 'lithe'. His face was too pink, his nose was a centimetre too long, and his mouth was two centimetres too narrow. He had heard his Auntie Maude say this. His hair was a shocking Irish-red that just would not behave, with or without gel. He had heard his pretty cousin Leah say that.

Ned also knew that there was no such thing as magic. Or at least he had not noticed anything wonderful about life at all to this point in his entire ten years. Oh sure Mom had read plenty of fairy tales and boy's adventure stories to him when he was a little kid. At the age of ten, he had been reading them to himself for quite a few years. But he knew that they weren't true. Or if they were real, they didn't happen to anyone as ordinary as he.

Now there was this little green glow in his garden. He kept looking, trying to focus his eyes through the greasy glass, but could get no clue as to what it was. He tried wiping the smudges from the window, only to find that they were on the outside. He used the binoculars that he got when he was five, but they were just baby binoculars that didn't magnify much. He stood up on the window seat to give himself a higher view which only made the tiny illumination look smaller still. He even attempted to open the window. It had been painted shut -- so no way he could un-stick the years of paint that had firmly sealed its seams. Finally, after all his failed efforts, Ned made a risky decision. He must go into the garden. He must see up close what was luring him from a distance.

So excited was he after making this brave choice, that he didn't even stop to change from his blue striped pyjamas. He just stuck on his moccasin slippers and, at the last minute, struggled into a light jacket. Then he crept silently down the side stairs so as to not awaken his parents.

When he got to the gate of the back garden Ned stopped, looked all about him. Maybe he should take Rufus with him for protection. Who knew what hid in dark corners? Rufus, the big, sloppy family dog was a Labradoodle, a Poodle-Labrador Retriever mix. He was as big as a Standard Poodle, almost big enough for Ned to ride. His blonde curly hair was flyaway, hanging over his eyes. Ned's parents had let the dog's coat stay shaggy and long with the overall effect of making Rufus resemble a woolly sheep before shearing. But he sure didn't act like a sheep. He was very bouncy; everything was of interest to him, particularly to his tongue.

Chapter One

Ned stepped carefully along the even edge of the patio, making his way in the darkness to Rufus' dog house, hoping to wake the dog quietly. Rufus had other ideas. Hearing the gate latch squeak, he was already on the alert and, seconds after identifying his human playmate, he'd jumped onto Ned ready for a game. Rolling on the moist night grass wetted Ned's pyjamas. Excited as he was, however, it didn't dampen his spirits.

Instead he tried to calm his canine buddy, whispering "Be still Rufus!" Sinking his fingers into the soft fur of the dog's neck, he began to stroke him gently. This was the fail-safe 'off' switch for Rufus' bounciness, as the dog would relax in concentration of the tickle. "We must be quiet dog", urged Ned. He kept up the tickle therapy on Rufus for a full five minutes before he encircled one arm around the dog's neck, lifted an ear-flap with his free hand, whispering into his friend's ear. "Okay boy, we are going to go for a walk up the garden. No noise, you hear?" As soon as he heard the word 'walk', Rufus jumped about boisterously demonstrating his joy at the notion.

"Oh no!" Ned winced, "That was a mistake. Forget that word! No, no, Rufus, not a 'walk', no boy." He sat down again beside the dog to calm him. This time when he made a move, he refrained from speaking. Instead he pulled Rufus alongside, as he began to sneak up the garden, his fingers laced firmly around the dog's collar. By the time they were halfway across the lawn, he found himself struggling to hold Rufus, wishing that he had taken the extra time to tie him to his leash. Rather than going back, he just held on tighter and within just two minutes, although it seemed like twenty, they were standing at the edge of Ned's patch.

There, just in front of his moccasin-clad toes, Ned saw the object of his curiosity. It looked like a clump of mushrooms, green mushrooms, with a slight glow to it, and a very soft hum. He had never seen a green mushroom in his life, never knew that they existed. What were they doing amongst his plants? Who could have had planted them there?

Unconsciously letting go of Rufus' collar, Ned shifted down to his knees to get a better look. His ten year old brain whirling into fully awake mode, he began his analysis. Why were they glowing? Why were they humming? Why were they green? And why, oh why, were they there in *his* garden? He thumped down onto his stomach to get an even better look. Their glow made them look more like a lamp than a plant. Also, they were definitely emitting a sound. Were they singing?

"Hello ... Thing," he whispered. By matching its sing-songy tone, he hoped to gain approval. "My name is Ned Clery. You are in my vegetable patch". All this was said slowly, clearly, just in case the mushrooms might understand. "May I please ... touch you?" At this the clump of mushrooms began to glow a bit brighter, just for a second, and the humming sound pitched a high note. "Is that a yes?" he asked, still in a hushed voice. The clump of mushrooms glowed brighter still, humming melodiously, as if in response. "I'll take that as a yes," he said, as the mushrooms sparkled and tuned again.

He reached his right index finger out, courageously inching his way forward. He wondered if it would feel like the mushrooms that he knew from grocery stores, a bit like slippery leather. At the last moment, he pulled back because an idea had just crossed his mind. "What if you are a toad-stool, not a mushroom? My Mom says those are poisonous!" The glow began to diminish; the clump stayed silent. "I'll take that for a no," he returned, as he poked his finger forward again. In fact, he certainly had no intentions of eating, or even of tasting. They were just too strange. Besides he was sure that they could understand him. So there must be something about them that was not plant-like at all. His finger lightly touched the cap of one mushroom. Instantly, the entire clump gleamed brighter than a Christmas light and sang more joyously than a Christmas carol! "Awesome!" squeaked Ned, pushing all his fingers forward in the darkness as he explored further.

In fact, these mushrooms were neither slippery nor leathery. They were cool and hard, and in their full glow, nearly transparent.

They looked almost like Mom's emerald ring which she always boasted cost a bundle. Could these be emeralds? Or could they be more valuable than Mom's ring? They were certainly much bigger.

"I think you must be very expensive," Ned concluded. "I must hide you or ..." Before he could complete this thought, Rufus had pushed past him, bouncing up to the mushrooms, licking them all over!

"No, Rufus, no! Leave them!" he cried, louder than he intended. To his horror, he witnessed the mushrooms go dark again. Grabbing Rufus' collar, he struggled back across the lawn with him and tied the dog to a rope affixed to the doghouse. Ignoring the whining protest, his heart thumping up into his throat, he raced back to the crystalline clump. In a panic he plopped down again, and with the shirt tail of his pyjama top, hurriedly wiped Rufus' lick off each mushroom thoroughly.

Lying back on the grass to catch his breath, he made another big decision, the second one in his young life – both of them on the same night! *Now I know I must protect you. What if Rufus gets off his leash? What if he eats you? What if ... What if someone should see you, should steal you?* It was with all these conflicted thoughts colliding in his brain that Ned raced to the greenhouse.

This particular greenhouse was Ned's very favourite hiding place. It was much bigger than a garden shed and full of wonderful treasures. Each spring Dad started his flowers out here on racks of metal frames. He would have flats and pots planted with hundreds of annuals and perennials of all shapes and colours. Every year the garden would get bigger because every year Dad planted more garden-beds. Ned only remembered the names of a few of Dad's plants: Shasta Daisies, Busy Lizzies, Johnny Jump Ups, Tiger Lilies. He remembered the ones with the fun names. Oh, and roses! He remembered roses. That was Dad's speciality. He had two garden beds dedicated to roses. Dad was a great gardener; he had what Mom called 'the gift'.

What got Ned interested in the first place in growing vegetables was that Dad grew tomatoes inside the greenhouse as well as in the garden. When Ned asked him why, Dad said it was a way of extending the growing season so that they could have fresh tomatoes up until the first snowfall. Ned hoped that he would inherit Dad's green thumb one day.

Most of the plants had been tucked into their outdoor garden beds by now, however. The only plants that remained in the greenhouse were those hothouse tomato plants and a few weaklings in need of Dad's intensive care. The small building was also used for storage. It housed all manner of garden tools, fertilizers, potting soil, mulch, watering cans, coiled up hoses, sprinkler heads – all you could imagine would be needed for the care of a great garden. And pots, dozens of them, all neatly stacked high on the shelves.

Throwing open the greenhouse door, Ned searched frantically around for the supplies that he figured he would need. First he found his very own trowel. Next he dragged a sack of enriched soil out from under one of the plant racks. Then he looked around for a pot big enough so that the mushrooms wouldn't feel cramped. He quickly scanned the shelves and chose one that Mom had bought when they had gone to Georgian Bay last summer. He chose it because it was big enough for the mushrooms to stretch out, pottery with watery-green waves which he thought they would enjoy. But mostly he chose it because it was on a lower shelf, one that he could reach without finding the stepping stool. Gripping his trowel tightly, he scooped out some soil from the bag.

With the filled pot and his trowel, he raced back to his garden. What relief he felt to see the green glow still there. The next bit would be tricky. He probed about the base of the clump testing for its roots, trying to determine where they were and how deep they went. Trowel in hand he started digging, pulling the earth away carefully, feeling for the ends as he went. He dug deep, deeper than he reckoned would be necessary; still the roots seemed to go on. As he scooped, his young gardener's hands were amazed at how extraordinary the tendrils felt. They also were crystalline, with bendable joints like strings of beads. In width they were a thick cord narrowing to sewing thread fineness at the tips. And they were tough. He dug deeper and deeper, until he had gone the full length of his trowel. If he stretched a little more, he figured, he might be able to dig further. He dug for a full half-hour and still he did not reach the root-ends.

It was only then that Ned did a desperate thing. Reaching both hands down to the bottom of the hole, he gathered together all the roots he could feel. At this depth, they had become thin indeed. Gripping as much of the threads in his hands as he could, he began to pull. Still they would not budge. What he did next Ned would later describe to himself as an act of madness. Almost without thinking he raged at it hard and fast, putting his whole body-weight into the effort. At last he felt the crystals loosen their grip on the earth. With a final force of energy, he felt their release. Flipping back with the clump held securely to his chest, he landed hard on the lawn.

As he lay on the grass, sweat beading on his face, streaming into his pyjamas, Ned gulped at the air. It was several minutes before he had calmed down enough to be breathing normally once again. And it was only then that he looked down at his prize. His heart ached to see the damage that he'd done. The gleam was almost gone from the mushrooms; their soothing hum had ceased. He had persuaded himself that he was protecting them from danger by digging them up. Instead he had exposed them to a greater danger still – his own stupidity and selfishness.

He took action immediately, frantic to save them from his rashness. Feeling along the lawn around him, he searched in the darkness for the pot. It was his toe that tapped it first. He flopped back down on the grass and, with caressing fingers, planted the crystalline mushrooms in the large pot, taking care to cover the roots with soil, tapping them into place. He then raced back to the greenhouse and placed them on the table where Dad stored his ailing plants.

Weak from his exertions, he slumped onto a stool, the hand of one arm on his forehead, the elbow on the table. He bowed his head, closed his eyes and remained like this for some minutes while he figured out what to do next. He had only planned this far ahead; from this point the way forward was unclear. He had no clue how to fix the mushrooms and less of a clue how to protect them. It was at this point, in the midst of his chaotic thoughts, that Ned heard the familiar humming. Opening his eyes, he saw a glow rising deep in the core of the crystals. When he dared to touch it again, they sparkled and sang to him.

"Were you scared?" he whispered, "because I was." The cluster glowed and hummed. "I'll take that for a yes", he returned, feeling all colours of guilt. "Can we still be friends?" he offered meekly. A glow and a hum. "Okay then, let's hide you", he said, looking around for a sneaky spot. He shifted the nursery pots around on the plant table to leave an opening at the back next to the wall. Placing the potted mushrooms in this space, he searched around for camouflage. Dad's gardening apron was hanging on a hook near the door. It would have to do for now. He didn't quite like to cover the clump completely with the apron. He would be more careful until he could determine what this wondrous new thing needed in order to survive. Instead, he folded the apron into a wall-like structure and placed it around the pot. Although a little brightness still showed, he felt that it was more or less safe for the time being, until he could come up with a better plan.

Ned then set about restoring the greenhouse to the way that he'd found it. He dragged the bag of soil back to the rack and shoved it underneath. He looked critically at the pot shelves, trying to remember how they had been arranged; pushing them around until he was fairly certain they were in the same places. Finally, he returned his little trowel to its hook.

It was only then that Ned could focus on a noise in the garden. It was Rufus whining loudly. Worried that the noise would awaken his parents, Ned quickly brushed the biggest bits of dirt from his wet, grubby pyjamas, grabbed for the door, stepping out into ... shockingly ... NOT his garden!

Chapter Two:
Lochamour Lore

The moon had vanished! This strangeness was only the first of a thousand details that differed between this scene and Ned's garden with a yapping Rufus in it. Yet most obviously, where seconds before there had been a silvery glow against a pitch dark sky outlining young roses, beets, and tomatoes, there was now – and this was most astonishing – there was now a faint golden hue reflecting onto to a watery surface, radiating upwards into a pale blue-grey sky, painting it with streaks of yellows, pinks and oranges. Wait ... *reflecting on a watery surface*? There had been no water in the garden! No pond, no stream, no puddle, nor even a sprinkler running just ten minutes ago!

What Ned noticed next, and heard, and felt, and smelled, made his feet come to a crashing halt and caused the bones in his knees to feel like they were dissolving into jelly. The water in question was a lake! The reflections on its surface came from rays of the sun just before it rose to touch the new day. Mist whispered up and vanished into the moist air. He could feel his feet lose grip on what was now much softer ground. A downward look revealed the cause. He was standing in wet sand, laced with reeds and wild grasses. Scanning the ground about him, he noticed some good-sized sitting rocks; he chose one now to sit and puzzle. From his vantage point on the knobbly stone, Ned took in the scene. He was on a beach of sorts, very close to the shore. To his left was a rustic hedge at the edge of a wood of evergreens, maples, oaks and small shrubs with all sorts of wild flowers growing in between. It smelled like a holiday. Or rather, the scent in the air reminded him of family vacations in the lake country. There was that familiar scent of pine in the air, mingled pleasantly with wood smoke.

Shifting himself left-ward to get a bigger sniff of the woods, Ned noticed for the first time the only familiar bit to this scene. Plunked onto the beach behind him was his greenhouse! Was it *his* greenhouse? Ned jumped up and peered into the windows. He could just make out the pots, the racks, and the tomato vines on climbing frames. So, did the greenhouse come along for the ride? Or perhaps was it he who had been the passenger on its ride. Did the greenhouse bring him to this very strange place?

The inside was just as he had left it. To be sure he checked the pots on the shelves, the array of tools lined up against the walls, and the nursery plants on the table, all in place. But something was awry. He just couldn't quite figure ... Then he saw it, or rather he didn't see it. He pulled away Dad's apron from around his recently planted pot. The crystalline structure had vanished! That was the correct word for it – vanished. It could not have been stolen. He hadn't moved ten feet from it. It was gone nonetheless. Ned looked around in confusion. Had it re-hidden itself? He poked around into every corner and cranny, but there was no sign that it had ever been there.

He kicked his feet hopelessly into the dusty floorboards and shuffled his way over to the window to watch the lake scene while he pondered. What he saw from the window was his garden again! How could that be? Maybe by returning to the greenhouse he had broken some sort of spell, and now had returned home. Maybe he was still asleep; would awake in his little bed in the morning after this great night's dream.

Once again he stepped through the doorway; once again he was back on the beach. He found his sitting rock again, this time jumping on top to get a higher view. It positively hurt his brain to figure out where he was, how he had got here, and why what he had seen from inside his greenhouse was so different from where he found himself now.

He would resolve the 'why' and 'how' riddles later, however. For now he would try to determine the 'where'. Looking down the beach in front of him, Ned spotted a cottage with lots of windows and porches, trimmed with twiddly bits of fancy cut wood. It may have been varnished at one time; now its wood finish was silvered and weathered. From what he could see from this distance, the cottage inside looked sleepy, although a dim light within hinted that someone was already awake. It had been built close to the lake's edge; a set of stairs led from its front door to a dock. The dock, made of log posts and timber, was greyed from harsh winters as well. It had been built onto flat rocks near the shore and continued some distance into the water.

A fluttering sound and a scuffling caused Ned's head to turn. A mother duck and her ducklings had waddled the length of the dock and were leaping one by one into the wet from a diving plank some two feet above. Forgetting all else, Ned relaxed into a giggle as he watched until the last duckling plunged after its siblings head first, then righting itself, paddled off. He kept them in his sight until they turned into black dots.

Now in the gloom of the half-light he could just see something bobbing up and down on the lake – a small boat. He crept forward to get a better look, taking cover behind the cedar hedge. With this closer vantage point, he could just make out the figure of a boy, about his age he supposed, dangling his legs over the gunwale of the boat, holding a fishing pole over the still water. Beside him was a dog in a half-sitting position, probably some kind of retriever, peering at his glassy reflection, his back legs quivering with excitement. An old man stretched out on the floor of the boat, perhaps tagging along for reasons of safety and to keep the boat in balance. A chain dangling over the edge of the craft was strung with six captured small fish. Ned sat down on the sand watching this pleasing scene in the early morning mist – the boy patiently waiting, his baited line in position; the dog with its ears forward, nose down; the old man nodding to sleep slumped low in the boat.

The suddenness of what happened next made Ned nearly leap out of his skin. The fishing pole bent almost in two; the fisher-boy let out a giant whoop! He jumped up, pulling back on the taut line, as he braced both feet to keep his balance in the now tippy boat. His dog let out a howl, bounding from the boat, paddling furiously in aimless circles. The old man jerked awake, shouting orders almost before his eyes opened. "Don't pull too hard or you'll break the line ... Take it slowly ... let it tire itself out ... Easy does it lad ... I got the net waiting for ya."

Ned stood up giving away his cover from behind the cedars, bunching his fingers into fists in his jacket pockets. His eyes held fast to the spectacle of the fisher-boy holding the line tight and steady against his lively catch. He could feel his own muscles tense along with the boy's. Finally, after what seemed to Ned like hours, the line slackened and the old man slipped the net into the water alongside the boat. He scooped the creature up, holding it flat against the side while the boy grabbed the oars and paddled back to shore.

The fisher-boy bounded onto the dock, quickly tying the boat's painter to a post while the old man still held the net fast. He then plopped into the shallows fully clothed. Taking the net from the old man's shaky hands, he pushed his subdued catch into what must have been some sort of underwater cage. He called his dog to shore, picked up the fish on the chain and helped the old man from the boat.

"Ya got a good 'un there lad!" praised the old man, thumping the boy's shoulders as they walked along the dock. "She'll be secure enough until after breakfast." As Ned watched, man and boy climbed the cottage steps, with the dog shaking the excess wetness from its fur falling into step behind them. Then before entering the dimly-lit veranda, Ned could just barely hear, "That'll fetch us a good price at market!"

Calm had been restored to the lake, yet the sun had still not shown its face above the horizon. "Wait, how could that be?" he said aloud to no one but himself, scratching his head for the hundred and tenth time. He was musing on this new puzzle when he heard a faint tone breaking the silence of the still air. It seemed to haunt the dawn, though he couldn't make out the words. He stood in silent concentration. It was definitely a voice, not a musical instrument that was tuning. It was pure, seemed to go straight into his heart, and it was so very, very sad!

Ned moved even further down the beach to bring himself into clear earshot. He was nearly next to the dock now, and although he could make out the voice, he failed to recognize the words. *The song must be coming from the cage*, he thought, *the fisher-boy's catch*! "I wish I could understand you," he said aloud. Moving closer still, as if lured by the sweetness of the tones, he suddenly began to make out the refrain...

Oh will you help me lad on shore
Will you set me free?
I am sad and alone in the dark
For my home I will never see.

I am a child of your lake lore
Will you set me free?
I am sad and alone in the dark
Oh boy, will you rescue me?

Ned ran forward and crawled onto the dock, keeping low to its timber surface. He slithered quietly in the direction of the melody. When he heard the line repeat, "Oh boy, will you rescue me?" he peered over the edge of the dock into what looked like a giant lobster trap. "Do you mean me?" he asked. "Am I the boy who will rescue you?"

A little head poked through the netting of the trap. It looked like a girl; still it was as small as a baby. "Oh, yes please," she said, her bright eyes streaming with tears. "If only you would!"

He reflected for just one more minute. Then, removing his jacket, pyjama top and slippers, he shoved them into a fissure between two rocks at the dry end of the dock and stepped into the lake, shivering as he pushed through the cold water. The trap was anchored a short distance away. Wading closer, he could now see the creature that had been caught by the fishing line. Her wet wavy hair was red like his, tied back with seaweed twine. Her skin was milky smooth with a faint blue tinge. She wore a skin tight top of a thin, sparkly fabric, the likes of which Ned had never seen. At her waist, she wore a sash of purple reeds and the fabric which covered her lower body seemed to be studded with red sequins of sorts.

"What were you doing in the lake?" Ned was going to ask, but he completely lost focus as he noticed a wiggly fish tail swimming around in the cage with her. When he looked closer still, he was flummoxed to see that this fish tail was actually attached to the child where her legs should have been. "Oh ... Oooo! Are you a mermaid?" he asked, his eyes wide as golf balls.

"Certainly not!" she replied in a high-pitched sing-songy voice. "Now that's just insulting!" Her tone softened again as she pleaded, "Will you set me free?"

Ned stood back, scratched his chin and thought deep thoughts. His ten year old brain framed the problem. Why would the boy and the old man capture this child? Why would they put her in this cage? To 'fetch a good price at market' the old man had said. But no one could own such a creature! Especially one who could talk! Why Mom had once said that not even Rufus was really theirs. She said they were giving him a place to live because animals, like dogs and cats, had no safe place to live in this world, except under man's protection. Besides, how many times did Ned feel 'sad and alone in the dark', as this being had voiced in her song? Then, of course, there was the red hair – just like his!

He looked about the cage for a latch, seeing none. "The anchor, I think", offered the child. Now Ned was a pretty good swimmer, loved the sport, but at this time of day it was so cold! Knowing that he must brave the chill, however, he dunked his head quickly to get the shock over and done. Then he sank down into the wet beneath, opening his eyes. Below the trap, attached to a chain, was a small anchor, lying far beyond the reach of the water-child. Ned swam down to the sandy bottom, dragging up the heavy anchor. A thick chain was attached to it at both ends with two metal clasps. By unlocking one clasp, he loosened an end. It was wound several times around a huge metal ring which held the trap door to its frame. With this free end, Ned untangled the chain from the rings and opened the door to release the child.

The tiny creature instantly grabbed onto his neck, smothering him with kisses. Then she swam far away from the dock, celebrating her freedom by swooping under the water and reappearing with a flip of her wonderful ruby tail. Ned could never explain to himself why he followed her into the lake just then – as he did. When he approached she giggled and splashed him, but she did not back away. *She likes me*, he thought. *Even with that man and boy playing a mean trick on her, she trusts me.* So he began to show off his swimming skills to her, throwing himself into the horseplay. He swam far out, half-chasing after her, diving under and shooting up to the surface as if he were part fish himself – that is, until a violent slap to the water instantly stilled their play. The fisher-boy, angered by the loss of his catch, had reappeared in his boat, spanking the surface with a vengeful oar. He flailed his weapon furiously, trying to connect with Ned's head, while Ned just as frantically tried to avoid being struck.

But it was the reaction of the water-child that startled him even more than the stabbing oar. She gave him another kiss, this time full on the mouth. When he opened it in surprise, she popped a pebble onto his tongue, grabbed his hand tightly, and dragged him under. She pulled him along with remarkable strength, swishing her tail so fast that they had descended to great depths before Ned had realized what was happening. He had expected his lungs to hurt. He felt sure that his mouth or nose would suddenly need to open to take in air. His lungs didn't hurt; his mouth and nose didn't open. He floated easily and weightlessly in the depths, actually feeling just a little bit better than usual. When his eyes had adjusted to seeing underwater, he could better appreciate his companion swimming around him in a kind of fluid dance. She came right up to him, cupping a webbed hand into a beckoning wave to follow her. It was not only the imminent danger of the boy in the boat, but also the thrill of the aquatic unknown that accounted for Ned's decision to go with her.

As they swam deeper and further, he could make out a series of entrances to caverns obscured by weeds. The water-child chose the widest of these openings, dragging him in after her. The way in was nearly blocked by a wall of fish – perch and sunfish, bass and pickerel, trout and pike – those were just the ones he knew. Oh and minnows! He loved minnows. When the water-child pushed up to this living barrier, it instantly parted to let them through.

Although he expected the cave to be dark, he found that he could see still with the aid of a light in the distance that travelled through the water to guide their way. Ned could just make out smoothed columns of rocks, standing about like statues. Lacy sea plants waved in the gentle currents. The water-child weaved around these columns enticing him to continue their game, which he was only too happy to do. They played in this way along the entire stretch of the cave until they reached the source of the white light. There in a brightly lit corner sat another water-creature, larger than the child, but still only the size of a five year old. She was curled up on a huge clam shell on a bed of seaweed. Her black hair was braided and pulled into a bun at the nape of her neck. She was quite delicate and her skin like the child's was a milky blue. In her open palm lay a very large pearl in its own shell shining like a lamp, illuminating the waters. It reminded Ned of his crystal mushrooms; he wondered for the hundred and eleventh time where they had got to.

This larger water-maiden turned angrily on Ned as he approached with the child. She waved him away, fluttering her tail furiously in his face. But the child swam up to her, circled her arms around the maiden's neck, singing softly into her ear. As she sang, the maiden's features began to soften. By the time the water-child had finished her song, the maiden was smiling kindly at him. All this while, Ned had stayed very quiet. He waited, perfectly still in suspension, until the maiden wafted over to him and kissed him on the forehead. Then cupping her hand as the child had done, she gave him a signal to follow.

They swam even deeper into the caves, the enormous pearl providing them with light. As it was a challenge for Ned's small feet to keep up with their experienced fins, the child pulled him along in her wake. After they had swum goodness knows how far into the depths, the water-maiden suddenly stopped and pointed up, starting to rise at the same time. Ned and the child followed.

To his great surprise they broke through the water's surface and found themselves inside an airy cavern. He took a clear sniff and found it quite breathable. Latching onto a smooth handle on one of the rocks, he pulled himself out of its internal lagoon. The cave was well-illuminated, astonishingly colourful. Throughout the entire structure, minerals of amethyst, rose quartz and green emeralds glowed, emitting a soft brightness of purples, pinks and greens. The giant pearl which the maiden had carried with them was placed beside them now, glowing blue-white.

On first glance, the cave looked like an enormous block of grey Swiss cheese! Its rock walls were full of large holes or 'pods' as he later learned they were called. Within each of these pods Ned could see beds made of seaweed topped with colourful fabric bedding, and tables made of driftwood, stone and shells. Colourful ornaments on seaweed stems hung from above; shell mosaics, woven cloth tapestries and sparkling fish-scale paintings surrounded each pod entrance. The glow from the minerals were magnified by these decorations, shooting soft beams all around the cavern, making it appear – magical – as indeed it must have been.

As he stared about in awe, Ned could sense eyes staring back. Having adjusted further to the soft lighting, he now focussed on the colourful water-people, lying or sitting about the cave and swimming in the small lagoon. They all looked much the same as each other, yet Ned could tell that they were very different as well. Their sameness came from the fact that everyone had tails studded with colourful scales. Their differences were defined by the colours of their skins, some of them matching their scales and hair -- blue, pink, yellow, red, and green seemed to be the most common – in many shapes, sizes and patterns. Yet they were all amazingly beautiful and wonderfully interesting.

Ned's eyes had only just begun to take in the details of the cave and its people, his ears had only just started to tune into the music, when the water-child splashed at him from the lagoon. "I know another game," she sang, luring him to the water's edge.

"Oh yes?" he replied with a giggle, "What would that be?"

"It's called *find the emerald*," she replied with a glitter. She threw a small green gem into the lagoon. "See?"

"Oh, I think I know how that game goes," Ned proclaimed, dive-bombing into the lagoon.

She easily beat him to the gem of course, but he didn't mind. It was the game that mattered, not the outcome. Each time they bobbed up again, he would try to grab it from her hand; each time she would yelp with delight and throw it beyond his grasp into the drink again. On his tenth attempt to retrieve the gem, his attention was suddenly snatched from the game by the water-maiden who had been his guide.

"Who are you boy and why are you here?"

Ned stared at her as he considered his answer, just for a moment. Before he spoke, he spit the stone from his mouth. It was a vivid blue colour, round and sparkling. He closed his hand tightly over it. "My name is Ned Clery. I am a ten years old." He pulled himself again onto a rock, then added, "I am a human boy, and I ... I don't know why I am here. I don't even know where *here* is!" Then, despite what the child had said before, and because he was so sure that he must be right, he thought he would ask again, "Are you a mermaid?"

"Ah, Ned Clery, ten years old, human boy, I know why you ask that question. You have heard of mermaids have you? We are not mermaids because, while we do live in the water, we do not live in the sea."

"These women here are called Chorda, Padina, and Dictyota", she said, indicating some delicate creatures lounging on the rocks. "They are fish herds and reed farmers. These men are Laminaria and Sargassum. They are the weavers of the beautiful fish scale and reed cloths that you have seen and admired around you. This is Halidrys. He is a food preparer." The men had been paddling about in the lagoon.

"My name is Alaria. I am the head of this podisphere, the keeper of the lore. And this," Alaria said proudly, "is Aqua-Marie, whose life you saved today from those very misguided humans! She is my daughter; she is learning all that I know, the histories and stories of our species. She will be the next keeper of the lore. She will inherit these duties when I am gone. You have saved her. We are very grateful."

"I've never before heard such fantastic names," said Ned, thinking how musical they sounded.

"We often take our names from our surroundings. Many of us are named after the plants that we grow. Some after the fish, some after the urchins..."

Ned turned to Aqua-Marie, as he now knew her name to be, who whispered, "I am not named after a plant. I am named after the reflected colour of the water under the daylight sky!"

"If you are not mermaids," Ned mused, "then what are you?" He scratched his head for the two hundred and thirtieth time.

"In your language we would be called lochamours," replied Alaria. "The term in our mother language, loch-tongue, is much more melodious of course. It would take you humans ten of your minutes to pronounce. We find that most humans have no patience to learn it. We live in deep fresh water lakes, not in salty seas. The female of our species, you may call lochladies, and the males, lochlads. This child," she said, pointing to Aqua-Marie, "is a lochlass."

Then slipping back into the lagoon to wet her tail, she asked, "Are you hungry?"

Ned had to confess that he was. He had no idea how long he had been away, but now his stomach was poking at his ribs. Alaria nodded to the lochlad swimming in the lagoon that she had said was the food preparer. He slipped onto the shore and pulled himself over to one of the rock pods, returning shortly with what looked like a raw fish stew served on a clam platter. "This is Halidrys' specialty dish," she said proudly.

"Why don't the lochladies do the cooking?" asked Ned, "My Mom does ours," he explained through a mouthful of the surprisingly delicious stew that he had scooped up with the tiny shell placed on the side of the dish.

"We may all perform all tasks as we wish. Our duties are not divided by gender or by age, but by skills, interests. In this way we best care for ourselves and for each other," said Alaria.

"That makes sense," mumbled Ned as he chewed away at his meal. Another thought suddenly surfaced, "What is this pebble?" He opened his hand to reveal the blue stone.

"That is very precious indeed!" Alaria replied in a hushed tone. "It is called an Indigo. It is solid oxygen. When you have it in your mouth, it provides your body with the oxygen you need to breathe underwater. Each lochamour is given one Indigo to hold for life. Although since we have gills," Alaria explained pulling back one of her ears to reveal their location, "we do not use them every day. In the winter, however, when the ice freezes over and the water itself is starved of oxygen, we hold them in our mouths while we sleep. In the spring when we awaken, we remove our Indigos, storing them until our next big sleep. You humans know nothing of solid oxygen of course. It does not exist in your world. Centuries ago, we learned how to distill liquid oxygen from the water; to press it into stone, stone as hard as diamond. We will sometimes lend an Indigo to a kindly human friend, of course, on the rare occasions when we invite them to visit. They must agree to keep them secret, however."

"Wow! Wouldn't it be great if you shared your recipe with humans!" returned Ned, with breathless enthusiasm, thinking of all the uses that people could make of such a gift.

"That we will never do!" Alaria stared darkly into his eyes.

Ned looked away quickly, concentrating on finishing his stew, trying to ignore that threatening look. The food made him feel strong and satisfied. He got to his feet in the hopes that he would be allowed to wander about exploring the cave just a little more. As fascinating as their tiny homes were, Ned could not take his eyes off the colourful walls. Those were both mythical and mysterious at once; their weaves seemed to be telling tales.

The lochamours were friendly and kind to Ned. But although they smiled, gestured and sang to him, they did not speak. Only Alaria and Aqua-Marie spoke to him in a language that he could understand. But this did not bother him. In his opinion, people in his world prattled on rather too much at times.

Soon he returned to where Alaria and Aqua-Marie sat singing to each other in their own loch-tongue. He lay back listening to the harmony contentedly. He was just beginning to nod off, when Alaria spoke to him again in his own tongue.

"Well, Ned Clery, what do you think of our home?" What words could he use to describe the wonder that he felt? Stupendous, fantastic, magnificent? There was not a word big enough. "W-w-well", he stuttered lamely, "It makes me very happy!"

As it turned out, this was just the right thing to say. "Would you like to know more about us?" Alaria offered generously.

Oh! He had so many questions. Did they live only in this lake or were there others? How many lochamours were there in the world? Did they all speak the same language? What else did they eat? Instead he said, looking up at the stone walls, "I love all these paintings and cloths on the walls. It seems to me that they are also stories, though I can't tell what they are saying."

"Ah, that is the best of all queries for these paintings, as you call them, are our libraries, our treasures. They are the lore of our world."

"Will you tell me the stories?"

"I will tell one," Alaria said, "but it is our most important one." Ned wiggled his bottom into a comfortable groove, sitting up straight and alert.

"First of all, I should say that we are nymphal, not humanoid as you are. Our species is magical, our lives are long. I myself will be five hundred forty three this season!" She laughed as Ned's eyes went wide.

"Next I should say that we did not always live in lakes. Once we had wings and lived on tree tops in large forests, where we flew very high in the sky."

"Were you fairies then?" asked Ned, his excitement rising.

"Not exactly fairies, no. There are more besides fairies that live in the air – although fairies are also nymphal. We are larger than fairies, smaller than mermaids. Also, our wings were made of feathers, not gossamer as the fairies' are."

She stopped at this point and turned to show him her back. "See where our wings were located?" She pointed to the slight indentations just off her shoulders. "This is where our feathers would have grown. They are not there now; still we could grow them again if we had to," she boasted.

"When did you lose your wings?" asked Ned, who by now had risen to his knees and was leaning forward in fascination.

"It was a great catastrophe a very, very long time ago. It happened when a giant asteroid crashed to earth. It destroyed many creatures, many species – burned our forests. As the forests burned, so did the wings off our backs. Those who survived took to the water. Fires burned for such a long time and, when they finally ceased, a deep, lasting cold set in. By this time we had grown gills and fish tails. As winged creatures, we had always weathered the winter by sleeping in the hollows of trees. Now as water beings, we sought caves deep beneath its surface, frozen by the longest, coldest winter of all. When the winter was finally gone, many of us unfroze ... and it was a different world!"

"Although the forests had returned, we were now more familiar with the lakes. So we stayed where we were. We had been water-adapted you see, yet we were as innocent as babies. We had to discover a new life for ourselves. We had to build new homes, find new food, build new societies and create new stories. All that you see around you Ned Clery is but 8,000 years old!"

"That seems very old to me", said Ned in honest surprise.

"When you consider that earth has been around for millions of years," Alaria explained, "it was just yesterday."

As Alaria continued her fascinating description, her melodic voice was slowly lulling Ned into sleep despite his great interest in the lore. Try as he might, he could not stop his mouth from opening into an enormous yawn. Alaria looked on him with compassion. "You seem cold; your trousers are still wet; you are very tired," she said kindly. "Look what Sargassum has woven for you while we have been speaking." Sargassum appeared on cue, holding a little costume out to Ned made of the lightest sparkling threads. "You may sleep in that pod over there in the bed laid out for you."

Ned did as suggested for he had to admit that he was numb with cold and wet, and his eyes bleary with fatigue. Removing his wet pyjama bottoms, he slipped on the fine clothing that Sargassum had prepared. It was very light, very warm and very comfortable. Next he slid between the two blankets on the seaweed bed snuggling into its warmth and, within seconds, was asleep.

The tugging of his blanket awoke him. "Wake up Ned Clery!" sang Aqua-Marie, "for you have slept too long!"

"What ... What?" he mumbled, as he tried to shake the sleep from his brain. "Why ... Why?"

"The day has not yet dawned," she said, panic rising in her voice.

"Then it is too early," he said, "I can sleep a little longer."

"No, Ned Clery! You do not understand. The day cannot dawn. You must go." Tears had appeared in her eyes.

"How can that have anything to do with me?" Seeing Aqua-Marie in tears made tears well up in his eyes too. "I didn't stop the day from coming."

"But you have dear boy," a calm voice behind him spoke. It was Alaria. "You are out of place and time. Now hurry, Ned, we must get you to shore. Use your Indigo; let us hasten."

He looked around for his pyjama bottoms which were nowhere to be found. He would have to go without them, wearing only his lochamour clothes. In seconds he was at the water's edge. Popping the pebble into his mouth, he jumped into the lagoon. Alaria grabbed for him and slung him onto her back, guiding his hands around her waist. She was away so quickly that he almost lost his grip. There was no pearl to light their way this time, but Alaria seemed to know precisely where to go in the darkness, twisting this way and that around columns of rock.

All the while they wiggled through dark waters at breakneck speed, Ned's mind was racing just as fast. Alaria had said that he was *out of place and time.* Aqua-Marie had said that he had *stopped the day from dawning.* If he had had a free hand to spare, he would have used it right now to scratch his head for the three hundredth time!

They arrived at the lake's surface much faster than they had descended just hours before. The sun was still pushing the top of its head against the line of the horizon, only whispering about a new day. *The day has not dawned*, he thought sadly.

Bobbing up to the surface, Alaria loosened his fingers from her waist and sloughed him from her back. He floated beside her, treading water, the tears returning. "The fisher-boy and his boat are gone for the moment," she assured him, "But you must go with all speed." She looked at him tenderly, "You are a good boy Ned Clery. You are loved by lochamours ... Now go home!" Her last words were delivered as she swished her tail into the air ... gone.

Ned watched after her while the water rippled and stilled. He was all alone once again. This time, as never before, 'alone' felt lonelier. Looking about him, he spied the dock near the cottage under which he had stuffed his jacket, pyjama top and slippers. He skimmed his way silently towards shore, watching the door of the cottage for signs of man or boy. When he reached the dock, he was astonished to find his clothes out waiting for him, including his pyjama bottoms – cleaned, dried, and folded. Another mystery he could not solve! Leaving his lochamour suit on (it was dry already), he quickly dressed. He spit the pebble into his right palm, shoving into it his jacket pocket. Then sitting down on the dock, he rocked back and forth, swinging both feet furiously. How was he to get home as Alaria had urged? His feet swung higher and higher. Would he ever see his own garden again? Would he ever see Rufus ... his parents? And, oh ... would the day ever dawn? All big questions, no smart answers.

Maybe if I stopped panicking ... started thinking. He dropped his head onto his chest and closed his eyes. Thinking was much better with his eyes closed. He could try to go back to the greenhouse, turn about and leave it again. Or maybe if he fell asleep in the greenhouse, it would be like going to another world and the day would dawn. Or he could ... nope, he had nothing. He sighed deeply and shut his eyes even tighter.

He smelled her first, that bit of sea-weedy scent. Next he felt her cold wet fingers touch his forehead. Opening his eyes, he saw her – Aqua-Marie, sitting beside him on the dock, swishing her tail playfully. Pleased though he was to see her, Ned couldn't help but panic as well. "You shouldn't be here! You will get caught by the fisher-boy."

"Never again," she replied. Looking very seriously at him, she added, "I promise." Her tone was sadly sweet as she sang, "I came to say good-bye, to give this back to you." She held up both hands over her head, grasping tightly onto a heavy object. It was the clump of green crystal mushrooms!

"Oh!" he cried with joy, "Where did you find it? I thought it was lost!"

"It was in the caves amongst our own lochamourian crystals," she revealed. "Magic attracts magic."

"So they are magic! I thought they must be, though I know nothing about them."

"I can only tell you a little. The rest you must find out for yourself. First of all, it is not really of your world, although it has found places to hide in it. It is called a Rhyll. It has amazing powers. Its magic is stronger than lochamourian magic! It brought you here, and it will take you home."

"A Rhyll," mouthed Ned, trying the word on for size. "Can it think ... feel ... understand me?" he asked, almost losing his breath in his excitement. Then he added, "Because I think it can."

"That I cannot tell you. That you must find out for yourself. Good-bye Ned Clery."

Ned grabbed for her arm, "Wait! You lochamourians say good-bye far too quickly." Then placing the Rhyll for the moment on the dock, he put his hand into his right jacket pocket and pulled out the blue pebble. "Alaria said that this must not be shared with humans." Reluctantly he held it out to her. "Thank you."

Aqua-Marie cupped his face in tiny hands, pressing her cheek against his. "It is my gift to you," she sang into his ear. "I know you will keep it safe." Jumping from the dock, she swished her tail gleefully to give him one final splash. "You will keep our secret, will you not?" she asked, but before he could answer she was gone.

Ned was laughing with tears in his eyes. "Yes, I will keep your secret," he whispered into the early morning air. Then, looking up at the struggling sun, he jumped to his feet, grabbed the Rhyll, and ran to the greenhouse. He knew just what to do now.

He opened the door, raced in and grabbed the pot in his free hand. Dumping some of the soil onto the table, he placed the Rhyll gently into the pot. Its roots were very clean from the water. It hummed happily and glowed brightly. "I'm glad to see you too", he said replacing the soil over the roots. Then sitting down beside it he said, "I should take you back to the garden." Instead he sat looking at the crystals for a few minutes more – for now he knew that it was called a Rhyll. Now he knew that it was magical. He needed a moment to get used to that.

"Nope, no good," he said finally, "It has to be done." Taking the potted Rhyll in his arms he pushed the greenhouse door open again and was back in his own garden. Rufus was still barking; the moon was still huge and blue; time had not passed at all; Ned was finally home.

He made his way in the dark over to his vegetable plot to where he had dug the hole. Placing the pot down, he dropped to his knees. He took the Rhyll from the pot, keeping as much earth next to the roots as possible, and re-planted it, filling in the hole and patting it down. Then he sat watching over it until the moon began to disappear and the sky to lighten. Returning the pot to the greenhouse, he carefully restored it to its proper place and sprinted back across the lawn to where Rufus was still whining mournfully. He tickled Rufus' neck a little longer until the dog slept again. Then he headed up the side steps to his attic room, weary from his travels. After dropping his jacket onto the floor and kicking off his slippers as he walked, Ned got into his very own bed. The blanket felt scratchy against his chilly body, but he fell instantly asleep nonetheless.

The sun was high in the sky when Ned awoke the next morning. He lay dozing, enjoying the warmth of a few more moments of sleep. All of a sudden he started up. He jumped out of bed and ran to the window. Nothing? He grabbed for his jacket, fell over his slippers, and raced into the garden, not stopping for Rufus, not stopping for anything. He plopped down in front of his garden patch and saw – nothing! No Rhyll. No sign that it had ever been there! He slumped back onto the lawn. Had it been a dream? It was all so real. If it was real where was the Rhyll? He sat back frowning, trying to remember. He must remember...

Sliding his right hand into his jacket pocket, Ned pulled out a blue pebble and held it up to the light. It sparkled indigo blue! He undid two buttons of his pyjama top, feeling just under the flannel collar for ... he found *that* too! Finally, he slipped the pebble into his mouth and lay back in the bright sunshine. His eyes looking towards the aqua-blue sky, he smiled ... and he remembered.

Chapter Three:
The Interesting In-Between

"This is the best fort we've ever made!" squealed Maeve as she helped Ned scoop out the sand trenches around his complex structure.

"It's not a fort, it's an underwater cavern," explained Ned, "and there's a lot more to be done. I'm going to need a ton of smooth pebbles for the columns," he instructed, "and shells for the furniture ... oh and some of those grasses."

***

Memories of the lochamours had woven themselves into Ned's dreams after that night and for a long time thereafter. In dreams he could feel himself gliding through water, descending to cool depths. In dreams, he could still sense the tickle of the wall of fish as they brushed past his body, while he was being tugged by Aqua-Marie through the hidden cave entrance. He could taste the stew served by Halidrys that only extreme hunger had even tempted him to try, but in the trying, he'd discovered a flavour so delicious that he wanted another bowl.

In dreams.

In waking life, Ned missed the lochamours and he longed for Aqua-Marie. He ached to play water tag with her, to hear her whispery songs, and to feel the touch of her cool fingers on his cheeks. So that summer, the summer of his eleventh birthday,

Ned positively tormented his mother by demanding repeatedly that she take him to the beach. A community pool was within easy walking distance. Still Ned much preferred the small beach at Island Lake, just minutes away by car. Although it was quite a shallow lake and certainly had no underwater caves, Rufus loved to chase sticks into its reedy waters, and Ned loved to swim and make elaborate sand structures. This summer, at his urging, they drove out to Island Lake at least three days a week. Although he was careful not to stay underwater long enough to panic his Mom, Ned took his Indigo with him each time, holding it in his mouth while he explored the shallows of the lake on his own.

It was at Island Lake that Ned met Maeve. She was nothing like Aqua-Marie of course. While Aqua-Marie was shy and whispery, Maeve was bold and loud. Even so, she reminded him of Aqua-Marie, being an excellent swimmer, both on and under the water. As they got to know each other, Ned began to like her more and more.

He first met her just as he was surfacing after a particularly long dive to find her peering into the depths with her face mask on, looking concerned. "Thank goodness kid!" she exclaimed, "I was sure you had drowned by now. I could just see myself having to dive under and pull your useless body to shore!"

She was tall for her age with strong golden limbs. The sun added pink cheeks to her pale face and bleached her blonde wispy hair. But it was her violet blue eyes that most caught Ned's attention, sparkling as they did like his Indigo. To him, Maeve was beautiful and he marvelled that she paid attention to a gawky kid like himself at all. He muttered something back to the effect of "No, no, I was fine. I like it under there," and then his words dried up. He had nothing to say. Wasn't it always the case with him, he thought sadly.

These few awkward moments didn't seem to discourage the young girl at all, who then offered, "I'm usually the only one diving here. I've been watching you for ages though. You never seem to need to come up for breath. Could you teach me how you do it?"

"Um, probably not," muttered Ned, ".... but I've found a great place under here with some really cool junk, like shopping carts and stuff!" he offered, trying to change the subject entirely. He knew of course that he could not tell her about the Indigo that he held under his tongue.

As it turned out, Maeve was a great diver and underwater swimmer herself. She could certainly hold her breath longer than most swimmers. But from that day, she became his swimming partner, then a sand constructor, and also a dog wrangler, as Rufus pushed his nose into their play. Ned looked for Maeve each time they went to the beach now and, although she was not always there, he had to admit that he enjoyed himself even more when she was.

On some of the days when they were not at the beach, Ned could be found in the reference section of the village library. He studied up on things aquatic – water plants, marine creatures, pests, predators. He grew concerned when he read about how polluted the lakes were becoming; he worried that it might force the water folks away.

Of course, Ned never forgot the Rhyll either. He had been so sad when it vanished, often wondered when, or if, it would reappear. Meanwhile he had not been idle. He became a bit of an expert on fungus, on mushrooms in particular. Although he doubted that the Rhyll was a fungus, he knew there was at least one common characteristic. They both sprouted in the darkness. He read that mushrooms grew best in rich moist soil, so just in case he kept the spot where the Rhyll had arrived clear of weeds, well fertilized, well watered.

Each evening Ned waited at that same window, and each night the moon waned a little more. It was inevitable then that two weeks after his Rhyll adventure, a new moon left the garden in pitch darkness. It was this absence of moonlight that got Ned to thinking that perhaps he should apply a little more science to his understanding of the who, what, why and when of the Rhyll. What if ... *What if* the Rhyll's appearance depended on the moonlight?

When he searched his brain thoroughly, he recalled the moon that night. It was full, huge and blue! What if the Rhyll only appeared on nights with a full moon?

The next day, Ned could be found again in the library, this time researching phases of the moon. He discovered that the moon was full every 29 days. Counting back, he calculated that the next full moon would come in 15 nights. It was a good theory, and one that Ned planned to test out. He made a calendar of the month of June and taped it to his wall. Each night he would watch for the Rhyll after his parents had gone to bed, and each morning he would cross off another night of disappointment. He pinned his hopes on that 29th night. As it approached, Ned got very excited indeed. That afternoon he packed a knapsack for the voyage, filling it with supplies he thought he would need: a warmish coat, Wellington boots, a long rope, a bathing suit, a towel, an extra pair of socks – and a peanut butter sandwich. Then he put his Indigo into the tiny leather pouch that he had made at day camp, and tying it to one of Dad's old work boot laces, hung it about his neck. The 29th night was so wet and foggy that he couldn't even see his garden from his bedroom window. He would have to actually wait in the garden, he reasoned. He went up to bed earlier than usual, but instead of putting on his pyjamas, he changed from his shorts to his jeans, put on a long-sleeved jersey and a pair of old runners. Then he waited quietly on his little window-seat until his parents had gone to bed. A full half hour after the light under their bedroom door had gone out, Ned picked up his knapsack and stealthily opened his bedroom door. At the last minute he packed his lochamour suit which he folded up into a tiny square, shoving it into his jeans' pocket, before slipping quietly down to the side door.

Leaving his knapsack just inside the door, he went to fetch Rufus from the garden. He regretted having to trick him, but after all it was for the best. When the dog jumped up on the boy, he clipped a leash to his collar and pulled him along to the mud room at the back of the house. He quickly shoved the dog into this room and shut both inside and outside doors firmly, throwing in a few treats so that Rufus' feelings wouldn't be hurt. Then he retraced his steps to the side door where he had left his knapsack. Putting on his raincoat and hat for the wet, he shouldered the bag and headed for the garden. So certain was he that this night would be *the* night, that it didn't even occur to him that he would be wrong. He sat patiently in his little corner of the garden. Then as hours passed, he began to wonder if perhaps the Rhyll might have popped up in a different spot. He scoured the garden for another hiding place. There was no sign of it – anywhere – as he waited, wetly standing by, until he saw the beginnings of the new sun.

***

After his disappointing night's watch in a soggy garden, Ned pushed all thoughts of Rhylls from his mind and determined to enjoy the summer fully with his new friend Maeve. Within a short while they had extended their time together at the beach to include such adventures as movie-going, bowling, and park games like *Rounders* and *21 And Up*. They became such fast friends, that it was not unusual for Ned's mother to invite Maeve to his eleventh birthday dinner about a month later.

"Sorry Ned", pouted Maeve, who arrived just after lunch on the day in question, "I'm bringing the rain in as well." So indoor play it would have to be for most of the afternoon. By early evening, however, the setting sun had finally decided to show itself just once before diving under the horizon; the grass in the garden was beginning to dry. Mom, who had grown a bit weary of having them underfoot, announced that she wanted some space to finish off the surprise bits of the meal, and she kicked them playfully out the door.

Ned and Maeve rooted about in the greenhouse, retrieving an ancient game of horseshoes which they decided to play on a clear patch of the lawn. They took turns tossing the horseshoes at their makeshift pitch, trying to catch the shoes around the stake. Now while Maeve was good at most sports, she really stunk at this game and Ned found that he was no teacher either. After one particularly wild toss, Maeve chased after her horseshoe into Ned's garden, and stopped with a sudden, "Oh! What's that?" bending down to peer closer at a shiny green object just peeking through the soil.

Ned, who had been lining up his shoe for what he knew was a perfect throw, stopped mid-swing and sprinted over to Maeve by the patch. *Argh*! he shouted inwardly, then outwardly "oh" in an off-hand tone as he secretly confirmed what it was. "Probably a bit of spinach ... or ... or you know ... celery?" He meant to sound more convincing, but an annoying question mark had crept into his tone that he was sure had given it all away.

"No," Maeve said frowning back. "No, I don't think so. I've seen spinach; I've seen celery.... Let's dig it up."

"No!" laughed Ned far too loudly. "I remember! It's just one of Rufus' old balls. He must have buried it in the garden, silly old thing." It was a lame lie and he knew it; so did Maeve.

"Ned .... Maeve! Dinner!" His mother's voice. Ned thanked his lucky stars, pushed a handful of earth over the green glow and hastened away, shoving his guest indoors before him.

Throughout the meal Ned fidgeted. He ignored his favourite dish of hot dogs with all the trimmings, barely tasting them as he wolfed them down far too quickly, causing his Mom to comment, "Is there something wrong with the 'dogs' Ned? I made them 'cuz they're your favourite." After this, a guilty Ned tried to look interested as Mom, Dad and Maeve, eating far too slowly, joked and told cute stories. He tried to look pleased when Mom praised his own lettuces that she had used in the salad. Once he tried to sneak from the table to peak through the kitchen window at his garden. Mom shooed him back into the dining room saying, "Secrets Ned!"

Secrets indeed! He was rocking a bit in his chair, thinking only of one thing. He had to positively force himself to look delighted at the vanilla chocolate chip cake with the chocolate icing and eleven burning candles that Mom walked in from the kitchen. The cake was fabulous, of course. No doubt one of Mom's best, and he told her so. The presents were perfect of course – a small telescope from his parents, a snorkel from Maeve. They knew him well. Or ... most of him. He made all effort to enjoy his party. He wanted to enjoy his party! He loved his parents and he was glad in the company of his friend. He really was! But he had stuff to do! He felt guilty that he wanted Maeve to go home *now*. However, just at this particular moment, he really did.

He was physically relieved when Maeve's parents arrived at last to take her home, and seconds after their car had pulled away, he was racing up the stairs to his room, mumbling "tired" and "thanks guys" as he dashed. Once in his room, he re-packed his knapsack and changed his clothes. This time he put on his lochamour suit underneath his regular clothes with the thought, *best to be ready if I'm going to swim with lochamours*! Then he alternately paced and peered from his window at the green light, now fully visible.

It felt like hours, but it was probably just thirty minutes, before Ned heard his parents' bedroom door click. Not even waiting this time for them to settle, he moved silently down the steps, taking just a moment in the kitchen to grab and wrap a piece of birthday cake before he was out the door and straight up the garden. He didn't even look in Rufus' direction. Beelining for his vegetable patch, he slid into position at the garden's edge. As before, in the exact same spot, was the Rhyll.

"Hello ... um ... Rhyll. Have you come to travel with me?" A hum and a glow.

"Wow!" he chirruped, racing to the greenhouse for the pot and trowel. His fingers were trembling as he prepared the green pot from before, filling it with soil. He was moving so hastily that he whacked the pot against the plant table as he turned to leave, a really hard crack that split it and spilled its contents onto the floor! He hastily grabbed for another pot, and scooping the earth up from the floor into this new one, he leaped out the door and up the garden again.

Chapter Three

Once back in place at the garden's edge, he paused for a bit of a re-think. Digging the Rhyll from the ground last time had gone poorly. He was sure that he had must have damaged it. There had to be a better way. "If you and I are going adventuring," he asked the Rhyll, "don't the two us have to first be in the greenhouse?" – a glow and a hum. "Hmm. Then may I please place you in this pot to carry you there?" A hum and a glow. With that the Rhyll struggled just a bit to loosen the soil around its roots, and slowly rising from the garden, settled itself into Ned's pot, wiggling into place.

"Ooooo!" Ned said in complete awe. "Too bad I hadn't thought of that before. Sorry about that." Then recovering himself and remembering his goal, he and the Rhyll approached the greenhouse together. Ned must not have noticed, as he pushed the door closed, that Rufus had sneaked in behind them.

Chapter Four:
The Tail of a Unicorn

Ned took a deep breath, turned around to face the door and slow-ly unlatched it. Then he nearly spilt over the threshold in shock as Rufus pushed past him, rushing out into tall grass, into field and after field of green blades, grains and meadow flowers, some of which reached above the dog's top notch, all of which stretched farther than the eye could see. It was a dog's paradise and Rufus was making the most of his freedom, racing about franti-cally, his head poking up here and there as he chased. "Rufus!" Ned shouted, "You sneak! You followed me? Rufusssssss!" he shouted again, although he knew it would be useless. What dog wouldn't ignore his master's voice with such temptation?

He stood in the doorway, surveying the scene. *So, not the beach then*, he mused, the head scratching beginning. *And I suppose the Rhyll is gone? Yup*, he confirmed as he looked back into the greenhouse. His next thought predictably was, I *have abso-lutely no idea where to go. But I do know it will include finding my Rhyll.* At this moment, a distant bark from Rufus jiggled a brilliant idea into his brain. "Rufussss!"

This time the dog answered, bounding up with his great tongue lolling out one side of his mouth. Ned reached back into the greenhouse for the pot and stuck it under the dog's nose. "Sniff," he commanded. Rufus stuck his nose into the pot, and took two deep snuffles. "Now, fetch Rhyll!" he instructed. Rufus let out a loud "whoot!" and raced off, his nose low to the ground.

Securing the pot in his knapsack, Ned grabbed it up and sprinted into the field in pursuit.

They headed in the direction of the full moon. *Well, that makes sense*, Ned thought. The grasses parted easily as they swished through. After they had been running for what seemed like an hour, Ned and Rufus stopped to catch their collective breaths. Now Ned could see landmarks beyond the fields. Off to the left was a grassy knoll covered with pine trees sloping onto a plain. But what was wonderful, and what caught Ned's attention, was that on this plain, a magnificent stallion was racing about, all black except for the silver outline painted by a brilliant moon. To his right he glimpsed a far off green light and he itched with curiosity. *It couldn't be the Rhyll*, he thought. Magic though it was, the Rhyll didn't shine this brightly at such a distance. Then, as if of one mind, Ned and Rufus started jogging in the direction of that light.

As they drew closer, he could tell that it was, in fact, a well-lit barn. It was certainly not an ordinary barn – not in the least. This one was framed with carved wooden posts and arches for stalls. But it had no walls. What was even more remarkable was that the roof's heavy wooden beams supported huge panes of thick glass through which the night sky twinkled. Great green globes of light served as beacons. As Ned walked about the barn, he met all manner of horsey creatures, resting under the shelter of this re-markable roof. Their coats varied from solid colours to patterns – black, grey, chestnut, and white. There were stallions, mares and foals, of course. But there were also mules, hinnies and donkeys, along with their young. Each creature roamed freely, nibbled grass and sipped water from troughs placed at intervals around them. In the rafters sat swallows, asleep in the night. Night owls flew about watchful for a midnight snack.

Ned would reflect at a later time, that he was always amazed, never prepared, whenever he encountered things mystical as he did at this very moment. For as he was scanning the glass ceiling, taking in the sight of swallows resting and owls flying, something quite dumbfounding flew past his view, something that made him rub his eyes twice and look again. There was a horse – in the sky! No, there were two horses actually, both flying about, one of them with a rider! The horses were pony-sized, sleek and blue-black; their wings, white and feathered, had a broad span. One winged horse seemed to hover over the field beyond the barn, while the other was doing air flips and rolls, a tiny person on its back. Although he couldn't be completely certain from this distance, Ned was also fairly sure that its rider also had wings!

"Wow!" he exclaimed, struck dumb with awe. Rufus must have been thinking the same "wow" because he didn't bark or even jump about. Instead he sat still on his haunches, jaw firmly shut, eyes fixed on the sky, his bounciness vacating his body for the time being. Horse and rider swooped about for a time before joining the other flyer in the field beyond, with Ned and Rufus following still in a kind of trance.

In the field beneath a drama seemed to be unfolding. A mare lay quietly in the grass, its foal whimpering at her side. As Ned and Rufus inched forward they could take in more detail. The mare was being tended by two nurses it seemed. One was a young girl, who stood by her head stroking her nose. The other, a mini creature with gossamer wings, sat on the mare's neck, cooing to her. Framing the scene were a stallion, standing silent, and a donkey, braying mournfully.

Ned and Rufus crept in closer, sure that they had not been detected until the little girl spoke without turning her head, "You have picked a bad time to visit boy. We are in a panic here."

"Oh ... hello," he said, moving into the open. "Um, is the mother horse sick?" he guessed from the concern all around.

"Tansy is restless, in pain, and we can't make her well. This is Buckthorn her mate," she said, pointing to the stallion. "Her foal, Rampion frets here by her side." Then as an afterthought, "That annoying donkey there is called Harrow. We wish he would be silent!" She looked sharply at the creature, which stopped braying instantly.

The girl turned toward him and now Ned could see her clearly. She had straight black hair, that had been pulled into two braids, and honey brown skin. She wore jeans and a tee-shirt much like his own, only instead of wearing runners on her feet as he had, she had on tooled-leather cowboy boots. As she was slightly shorter than he, Ned guessed that she was perhaps a bit younger.

"And your name ...?" started Ned, prompting her response.

"I'm Sierra. This is my friend Bellflower. She usually rides her horse Nightmare who is waiting for her in the sky. Black Thorn waits beside her up there, with Bugloss on his back."

Bellflower was no bigger than a chipmunk although, except for those wings, she looked human like him. Her long hair was a buttercup gold and fell loosely onto her shoulders. She had translucent gossamer wings that seemed to reflect the moon's glow. She wore a simple costume which clung to her body, the colours reminding Ned of wild flowers.

"Are you a fairy?" he dared to ask.

"Of course, simple child!" she said hotly, "What else would I be?"

"I got it wrong once before," he explained, finding it impossible to take his eyes off her. "You are my first fairy."

"Rude," sniffed Bellflower, "rude!"

"What's rude?" Ned asked, backing away just a little.

"You are, with your ... your staring!" she retorted. "Your dog is sniffing me too! Rude, rude!" she cried again, fluttering her wings at Rufus' wet nose. Ned pulled Rufus away, turning his attentions to the mare.

He dropped to his knees in front of her, feeling her forehead. In truth he didn't know how hot it should be, though it was warm to the touch. He did what he remembered his mother would do when he was sick; he didn't really understand why. Beyond this he hadn't a clue.

"Can't you give her a pill ... or syrup?" he suggested, remembering the colds and flus that would keep him in bed.

"I think it's more complicated. I think she may have eaten something she shouldn't, like deadly Nightshade. I'm not sure what it was. We live hundreds of miles from any animal hospital. I have tried all that we have here to neutralize a poison like this – all the lotions and potions on Father's shelves," Sierra replied, pointing to a dozen half-full bottles of colourful liquids that lay in the grass about her feet. "Nothing has worked."

"Can't your father make up a new medicine?" Ned suggested, growing concerned at the animal's distress.

"He would know just what to do if he were here. But he is miles away, gone to pick up a wounded stallion. He hasn't heard that Tansy is sick, and he won't return until tomorrow. Then it might be too late!" she said, a tear escaping one eye.

"You can't be here alone," Ned observed. "Someone must stay with you when your dad is away."

"Oh yes, Granny Nadie lives with us. But with her creaky legs, she can't walk the fields anymore. She would try though, if she heard about Tansy. No, I have to find a cure on my own."

"Not on your own, dear child," murmured Bellflower. "I will not leave you while the mare is ill."

"Aren't fairies supposed to be magical?" asked Ned.

"Rude! I have tried what I have in my larder."

Ned gently stroked the mare's back as she slumped further down on the grass. This was obviously a close-your-eyes-and-think moment. He rested there searching for just a smidgen of wisdom, his silence only disturbed when Rufus began whining, pawing at the ground nearby. Crawling the few feet to where the dog was prodding, Ned found his Rhyll lying on top of the ground between two clumps of grass.

"Aha!" he shouted, "Here's where you've got to!" He opened his knapsack, retrieved the pot, and snuggled the Rhyll into it.

"What you have there is quite magical boy," the fairy observed, her eyebrows arched highly. "Perhaps you are not as boring as you seem. Who are you then? Where do you come from? Why are you here?"

"My name is Ned Clery. I come from my house in a village. I keep being asked that last question, but I don't know why I am here ... And I think you are rude," he added quietly.

With his potted Rhyll in his arms, Ned found that he could think much better. A few more moments are all that it took for a half-formed idea to occur. The logic of it only seemed to gel while he was speaking, "You said that you had tried all the potions in your larder," he began, "Are there potions that are not in your larder that could still be tried?"

Bellflower flew over and sat on Ned's knee, sitting in quiet reflection. "Perhaps ... perhaps!"

She flew up to where her winged steed awaited, and they took off into the night. It was just a matter of minutes before she returned with a dried petal in her hand. "Here it is!" she cried. "Oh, I had such a time finding it. I looked under my toadstool chairs and tables, sorted one by one through my dried flower collection, tossed all of my twig desk drawers upside down, looked in and under my leaf bed. Could I find it? No! Then I suddenly thought. Ninny! Grandfather had it last. It must be in a hidey-hole of his. So I searched all the tree knots for a mile or more. Then ... there it was!" She smoothed her hands over the petal's surface.

"There what was?" asked Ned and Sierra together. They were more than a little amused by Bellflower's description of her long search, especially given the fact that she had returned almost before she had left!

"The recipe, of course!"

"Of course." Ned and Sierra exchanged smirks.

"Right! I have never made this before, but I have seen my grandfather do it, so I think we will be alright. We will need to multiply the quantities, by a hundred times or more I should think, to adjust for the mare's body weight. Hmmm ... we will need:

Feverfew – that's a meadow flower, which will be easy.

Rabbit spit – we'll get that off my friend Myrtle.

Gentian – an alpine flower; I don't have any in stock; we will need to go the foothills for that.

Bee's wings – I might have a couple in stock, from what I have found lying about in the meadows.

Morning dew – I have lots of that because I collect that everyday.

"Oh! ... Uh-oh. This could be a real problem."

"What?"

"*Big* problem," nodded Bellflower, "with the last ingredient ... *Five hairs from a unicorn's tail.*"

"Yipe," said Ned. "I didn't know unicorns existed. Then I guess I didn't believe in fairies until a few moments ago."

"Oh they exist," affirmed Bellflower. "Problem is ... where?"

"Then we are back where we started," moaned Sierra. "Tansy will get worse and then ..." Her voice trailed off.

With the Rhyll still in his arms Ned was looking very grim. Then, "Hang on just a minute! A friend once told me that 'magic seeks magic'. The Rhyll is magic. The unicorn, I presume, is magic too. Couldn't the Rhyll find the unicorn?"

"Brilliant idea Ned Clery! Top of the class!" proclaimed Bellflower in her taking-charge voice. "Here is what we will do ... Ned and I will search out the ingredients, Sierra and Bugloss will stay with the horse and ..."

"Wait! What?" replied Ned. "You want me to come?"

"Oh yes you must come. You have the Rhyll. It is your friend, not mine. Besides, I cannot carry a hundred times the quantity that this recipe calls for. It would take me days ... Well?"

"When you put it like that, I guess I must come," Ned admitted, "But you sure are a bossy boots!" A list of worries scrolled through his mind at this point. How useful would he be? Could he travel as fast as she? Would he figure out how to read the Rhyll to find a unicorn?

He started pulling out his boots, socks, swimsuit and towel from his knapsack, leaving them on the grass. He repacked his warm coat, the length of rope and the birthday cake. To this he added the pot of Rhyll. Then he pulled the flap loosely over, securing it about his neck. "Ready ... I guess," he said without conviction. "Come on Rufus, let's go!"

"Oh, no, no, no, no!" cried Bellflower. "That dog must stay here. We cannot take that dog along!"

"He'll behave. He's getting better all the time at heeling and staying!" Ned defended his companion vigorously.

"Not the point, I am afraid," returned Bellflower, "The distance is so far that we must ride on Nightmare. Nightmare will not allow any dog on her back. Anyway, that dog could not keep his balance. Besides, I hear that unicorns are very shy and must be approached gently. They need to be persuaded to give up even a few of their hairs."

"Leave Rufus with me," offered Sierra. "I'm staying with Tansy anyway. I'd enjoy his company."

"I guess ... it's all settled then," Ned agreed. "Is that flying horse what you called 'Nightmare'? Spooky name, by the way."

"Perfect name if you ask me," retorted Bellflower. "She is a mare and she flies in the night! Now get on. We must not waste any more time."

Ned climbed on the horse that had dropped to the ground to receive him. He shifted into position behind Bellflower, turned his knapsack onto his back, and held tightly to Nightmare's mane. The power behind the take-off pulled him back, nearly forcing him to let go. He could feel the wind ripping at his hair and clothes as they raced through the dense night air. Once his panic subsided,

Ned could relax, even enjoy the flight. It was a unique opportunity after all to fly above the world, on the back of a winged creature as splendid as this no less!

The ground below was blackened by the night. Still he was amazed by the beauty of the light clusters outlining the small towns and villages they passed over. Most of the lights were tiny and twinkly like the distant stars. But there were spotlights as well, powerfully bright, that shot shafts of light into the darkened sky. They travelled through clouds, brushed over trees, avoiding the occasional pointy hilltop.

Ned marvelled at how quickly Nightmare flew. At this speed they were bound to arrive there in no time, wherever 'there' was. Suddenly Bellflower tugged at the mare's mane, "Whoa girl! You must rest." Nightmare halted mid-cloud, hovering inside the wet fluffy mist. She lapped away at the thick wetness with her tongue as if it were a water-trough. Bellflower did almost the same. She reached out to pull a little foam into her hands, offering it first to Ned. He breathed it in and found it more refreshing than anything he had ever drunk.

As Bellflower sipped her piece of cloud, she grumbled, "I do wish I had thought of a snack. My tummy is rumbling."

"Mine too," agreed Ned, then "hold on ..." Opening his knapsack, he found his piece of cake.

"What's that?" breathed the fairy, peering at it in wonder.

"It's birthday cake," Ned explained, "My mom makes it best. Try it."

Bellflower pulled a tiny piece off, a few crumbs of cake and a chocolate bit, just touching it to her weeny tongue. After that first lick, however, her tongue moved faster around the sweet morsel, licking it smaller and smaller until it was gone. Then she lay back on the horse's mane holding her belly, a look of pure satisfaction on her face. "Mmmmmm! That just may have been the most delicious treat I have ever tasted." She closed her eyes for a few moments to savour the flavours that remained in her mouth.

"Yup," Ned mumbled through a mouthful of cake. "Told you my mom's is the best."

"Do not eat it all greedy boy!" Bellflower demanded. "I may want some more later."

Ned smiled at the sauciness that he had come to expect from her. As soon as he had wrapped the rest of it up and closed his bag, they were off again at full speed. It wasn't too long before Bellflower delivered new instructions into the horse's ear, that then dropped to the ground in a meadow surrounded by mountain peaks. She jumped off, sniffing the air a few moments before she declared, "This way I think Ned." He followed her up a steep hill to a patch of delicate flowers, deep purple in the moonlight. "About twelve of these Gentians I should think," she declared, "Put them carefully in your bag."

After doing as instructed, Ned climbed onto the horse again. "That was pretty easy," he observed, "We should be back in no time."

"Maybe not," she replied. "This next bit is the tricky one. It is all up to you. Now you must find the unicorn!"

Ned opened his satchel and pulled out the pot. "Could you please tell us what direction to take Rhyll?" he asked it politely.

"What?" scoffed Bellflower, "We have no time for please's and thank you's!"

"I think most creatures respond better to a kind voice than to a shout," Ned defended, "most especially my Rhyll." He held out the Rhyll to the east, west, south and north. At the first three directions the Rhyll remained unchanged. When his hand faced the north, however … a hum and a glow. "It's this way," he declared. They were off again.

The horse headed north, flying higher to avoid the snow-capped peaks of the mountains. The Rhyll glowed bright when they headed in the right direction, dimming as they veered off course. In this way they found a way to proceed, Ned tugging Nightmare's mane left and right according to the Rhyll's reactions, until at long last he cried "Stop!" near the crest of a huge peak. The Rhyll was thrumming loudly; its gleam sent spots before Ned's eyes. "This must be the place," Ned announced, confident in his Rhyll's advice.

"Nightmare cannot land here," Bellflower announced, "The peak is too slippery and sharp. She will lose her footing. I can fly down to find the unicorn myself, I suppose, you being without wings and all."

She was gone only minutes before she returned in a huff. "That will not work," she declared. "Stupid unicorn! We must go without! Away!" She squeaked to a startled Nightmare, who made ready for flight.

"Wait!" Ned protested, pulling back on Nightmare's mane. "You can't just ... just give up. Can you? Can we?" his voice ascending to a higher questioning point.

"It is no use," declared Bellflower. "Who knew unicorns were so rude?"

"Okay," returned Ned in a reasonable voice. "Did I understand right that you found the unicorn?"

"Oh yes, one was there. It flatly refused to give me one hair from its tail! Rude!" she cried out with a tear of frustration.

"Now," he whispered, "Just who was ruder? You or the unicorn?"

"Maybe .... Me," Bellflower confessed.

"Right then," said Ned, "I must try I suppose. I don't know quite how, but ... Grabbing the length of rope from his knapsack, he tied one end securely about the horse's neck and the other around his own waist. Then sliding over the animal's back, he inched himself downwards, until he could feel ground.

Next he removed the rope from his waist, leaving it dangling in place. He carefully crawled around the slippery shelf peering about him as he went. Boulders of snow twice the size of him were crowded onto that ledge. Piercing these boulders were dozens of huge icicles like unicorn horns, shooting upwards and outwards with needle sharp points. They marked the entrance to the unicorn's home for a fellow unicorn, while at the same time, discouraged invasion from an unwelcome visitor.

Not daring to stand in case he should slip, Ned crawled about until his knees and hands felt quite frost-bitten, his runners filled with snow. He found a way forward by weaving around the boulders' spiral pattern, ducking under icicle spears on the way. At the end of this weird maze he came to what was unmistakably the entrance to a cave. Distance-wise it was not far from his dangling rope.

He had just put two knees past the cave's entrance when he saw what he was looking for. A unicorn! This was not the unicorn that he had read about in stories, however. This one was pure silver in colour and gleamed like his mother's candlesticks. It was, in truth, the most majestic creature that Ned had ever seen. Its horn sparkled like diamonds, its mane and tail flowed like silk. Its eyes flashed like sapphires, its teeth like pearls. When it showed its teeth, that is, which it did at this moment, rushing fiercely at him, forcing him away from the entrance.

He stepped back, stumbling against the shards of ice, walking backwards around the balls of snow. He was so watchful of the unicorn's horn that he failed to notice how close he was coming to the sheer edge until he had slipped straight over! His knapsack flew into the air. Unlike Ned, however, it landed on the ledge, the Rhyll spilling out. He only just caught onto the dangly rope in time or things could have turned tragic in an instant! Swinging about on the cord, he held on with all his might, blowing onto his frozen fingers to warm them enough to pull himself up to Nightmare's back. As icy as they were, however, they froze to the rope. Up above Nightmare rutted the air, causing the rope to swing more erratically and Ned's hands to slide down even further. Bellflower began to scream from above Nightmare's back, which only added to his fear and confusion.

Meanwhile, the unicorn had followed him onto the cliff. He was terrified to think that it might bite off the rope. It stopped short of the edge, however, looked down and sniffed at the Rhyll, resting the tip of its nose in amongst its caps. The Rhyll hummed and gleamed like never before until the unicorn at last made a move towards Ned. He tried to reach for a lower piece of rock to avoid its wrath. But instead of gnawing at his lifeline as Ned fully expected, the unicorn held out its horn for him to catch onto, pulling him back to the safety of solid ground.

He lay panting against a boulder, shaking from panic and cold. Pulling his bag open, he retrieved his warm coat, pushed both arms in, and zipped it to the neck. "W-w-why? W-w-what?" He spoke breathlessly, reaching at the same time for the Rhyll.

"I thought you were another of those annoying verdi-fairies," said the unicorn. "They buzz about shouting orders! They make my tail twitch. But apparently you are a Rhyll-friend. It tells me that I must give you an audience."

"Oh ... you can speak? And you understand Rhyll? I am only just learning the language myself. ... You're different than I expected," Ned observed, gulping back his wonder.

"Ah, you have been reading fairy stories I suppose," replied the creature. "They are full of mistakes. They say that our horns are magic. And, while our horns do hold our own life-force, they are magic to no one but us. Other bits of us are magic, I suppose, though we do not share these anymore."

"I can see your point of view I guess. Still I do need your help. I am Ned Clery – just an ordinary boy really. I am on a mission of sorts. Bellflower the fairy, the verdi-fairy as you called her, may be rude but she has a good heart. She is trying to make a medicine to help a horse that just may be dying. Isn't a horse like a cousin of yours? I have come along as her assistant; also because the Rhyll is my friend," he ended weakly.

"Hmmmm. Let me consider ... My name is Argentian by the way," the unicorn said, completing the introductions. "I am a fine example of the male of my species. I am the guardian of this gate. You want hairs from my tail I suppose?" He stood silent for a full minute. "If .... *If* I should give you some, what can you give me in return?"

"I have a warm coat, a rope, birthday cake. Those are mine to give." Ned offered, keeping hidden his lochamour gifts.

"Oh I don't want your gifts," Argentian replied. "I do love a good story though! Are there any good stories in you Ned Clery?"

Ned thought for just a second before he replied, "I guess, since you are also magical, I could tell you about lochamours."

"Just what are lochamours?" Argentian replied, his eyes sparkling with interest.

So Ned told the unicorn of his adventure with the lochamours – about rescuing Aqua-Marie, about their colourful bodies, their seaweed fabrics, their wonderful underwater caves and lagoons, and their fascinating customs and lore. He described the actions of misinformed humans towards lochamours; how he was ashamed of their ignorance. There was one thing he did not mention, however. He did not tell Argentian about Indigos. That was a solemn promise.

Ned came to the end of his narrative, his voice trailing off. In the silence, he could hear and feel the wind whipping around the mountain peaks, increasing the chill to his skinny limbs. He sunk lower into his coat with his head under the collar, shoving his hands deeper into its pockets.

Once he did speak, Argentian's powerful voice pushed back against this wind. "You do tell a good story young Ned, one that I had not heard. Shall I tell you one in return?"

"Oh, yes please," replied Ned. Although this was taking a great deal of time and he was desperate to return to warmer altitudes, Ned felt that the unicorn needed humouring still. Also, he did enjoy a good story himself, he had to admit.

"In the past," began Argentian, "we too have been badly treated by creatures who wished us ill. They were greedy for our gifts – our tails, our blood, the sapphires they thought must be in our eyes. They mostly wanted our horns though because they thought it would make them live forever. But they could not live forever with our horns, and sadly we could not live at all without them. Many of us died at the hands of such brutes, until one day the few remaining unicorns came together for a council. At this council they decided to leave the company of these greedy creatures to find a place of safety.

For years they searched for a new home where they could not be disturbed or hunted. At last, by the greatest of fortune, one of our clan discovered a cave entrance at the base of a mountain, hidden from the view of all but the most observant of creatures. Mankind, as you know, is not always observant. This ancient kinfolk of ours, Luminar was his name, explored the cave thoroughly, searching through tunnels, marking his way as he went, climbing all the way up its steep slopes to the mountain top. Most importantly, Luminar found huge theatres of space right within the mountain that could be planted in pastures. What made it perfect was that both sunshine and rain still entered these spaces through the many shafts in its steep walls. At the same time the outer walls would be too hazardous to be accessed by human climbers. It was the perfect refuge for us. We move into that mountain centuries ago."

Then Argentian looked very solemn indeed, focusing his eyes upon Ned, "That mountain Ned Clery is the very one on which you now sit. You sit at its uppermost door! You have discovered our centuries' old secret, you and that pesky verdi-fairy that is."

"I do see what you mean," Ned admitted. "You wonder if I'll tell your secret. Well, I am keeping secrets in my heart already. I am sure to have room for one more. As to where you live? I have no idea where I am. How could I ever return or direct anyone here? Bellflower is no threat to a unicorn either – no more than a horsefly I should think."

Argentian stared at Ned for some minutes, searching his face for the truth of his claim. Then pulling a few hairs from his silvery tail, he placed them on Ned's fingers saying, "There should be enough – in fact more than you need in that tuft. Do not let that obnoxious fairy have more than she actually uses for the medicine though. You must keep the leftovers for yourself — because you never know ..."

Ned thanked Argentian profusely. Of course under different circumstances he would have asked to stay longer, but his path on this night was all too clear. His presence in this place and time was affecting the dawn. A bit reluctantly he restored the Rhyll to the bag, climbed back up the rope and onto Nightmare's back once again. "Okay, now we can go."

Bellflower was clearly impressed. "You have the unicorn hairs?" Ned simply nodded. "Right then," she proclaimed, back into bossy business mode. "To my meadow I think Nightmare, where we'll gather the remaining ingredients."

On the long return journey Ned talked close to Bellflower's ear so that she could hear his voice over the roar of the wind. "The unicorn, Argentian his name was, called you a verdi-fairy," he said, "Is that true?"

Grabbing his neck to turn herself around, Bellflower replied, "Oh yes very true, though I am surprised that the unicorn knew it. We verdi-fairies live in meadows to look after the flowers, grasses and grains. We water them daily with dew; we carry pollen from species to species to help them flower and seed. We even tuck them in bed for the winter, before we hibernate ourselves. Verdi-fairies make the best of friends, especially to those who honour the land, as Sierra and her father do."

They spent the remainder of their homeward flight distracted by their conversation. Bellflower told Ned about the sanctuary, with Sierra and her father as caretakers. She told him more about their refuge for animals living wild that occasionally needed their help. She related the stories about how they provided shelter from rough weather, found cures for ailments, offered the occasional change of diet. It was a place where animals of all kinds met up; where all seemed to respect each other. Amazing indeed! Ned sniggered as she described Sierra and her habit of naming all their guests after the flowers of the meadow, there being a great many of those.

They were so wrapped up in their talk that neither boy nor fairy had noticed that Nightmare had flown straight on without stopping. She had found her own way back to the meadow. Startled into action, and team-mates that they had become, they quickly pulled together the final bits for the recipe. Bellflower showed Ned where to find Feverfew – lots would be needed. She herself dashed quickly home for the bees' wings – all that she had in stock. Then they searched out the rabbit named Myrtle who obligingly spit onto a flower petal. They placed this in with the rest in Ned's sack.

Finally Bellflower brought Ned to a trough near the barn which was filled with her extra stock of morning dew. "Since we can't move the trough," she observed, "We will just have to make it here."

Sierra and Rufus greeted them well, as if they had been gone for months. Rufus' bounce had returned in full force. "He just stared at the sky the whole time you were gone," claimed Sierra. "I told him you would be back but I don't think he believed me one bit."

Sierra ran to the barn to fetch the tools they would need – a mortar and pestle that her father used to grind herbs, and a bucket to make and carry the liquid medicine for the sick horse to drink. She and Ned ground, measured and combined the ingredients to Bellflower's barking orders. As Argentian had instructed, Ned snuck three leftover unicorn hairs into his jeans pocket, after all that would be needed had been measured out. When the concoction had been mixed to Bellflower's satisfaction, they carried the heavy bucket together to Tansy's bedside. Lifting her head, as she was much weaker now, they encouraged her to drink.

The horse drank half of the bucket's contents before she laid her head back down again. Her nursing staff stood anxiously by.

After waiting what seemed like an age, Sierra then felt the mare's forehead, passing her hands over her back and chest. "Well, she's not shaking as much, but she is not recovered enough either," Sierra observed, "She still looks fretful in her dreams. The medicine has helped, but it has not cured her."

With hands on foreheads, elbows on knees, they all sat around thinking, searching for answers. Suddenly Ned leapt to his feet, a remarkable thought entering his head. He ran back to the water-trough where he left his knapsack. He opened it briefly, with apologies to the Rhyll, "Sorry that you have to travel like baggage." Then he carried the sack back to the field to where the solemn group still gathered. There he removed the Rhyll from the bag, saying almost breathlessly, "May I?" A hum and a glow.

He picked the Rhyll up carefully, shaking the soil from its roots as best he could. Then he walked over to the half-filled bucket, adding the Rhyll to the potion while the others looked on with open mouths. "I know for a fact it can swim," he explained. He left the crystals submerged for a full five minutes before he reached in to retrieve it. "That should do it," he proclaimed. "Let's get the rest of this into her."

Although the sick mare protested and struggled a bit, she drank the potion right down to the bottom. Seconds seemed like minutes, minutes like hours, then ... She struggled at first; she fell back again. Then with a final push, Tansy was on her feet!

A moment of silence before the outburst of voices, humans and creatures alike. Bellflower shouted loudly, skipping about a twirling Sierra. Buckthorn the stallion was snorting and pawing the ground. Harrow's braying was joyous now. Even Rufus chanced a bark or two, and Ned let out a yip. The Rhyll? It put on a light show that every creature stopped to enjoy.

As the noise tapered off, Ned sat back on the grass, his heart resting somewhere between relief and satisfaction, as he watched Tansy walk about gaining strength with each minute. He witnessed her and Buckthorn nuzzling noses, as Rampion whinnied and snuggled against her once more. He tickled Rufus' neck saying, "Good boy!" Then he re-potted the Rhyll whispering, "Thank you".

Finally he heard the fluttering of fairy wings just before Bellflower dropped right down onto his head. Sliding over top of his forehead, she winked as she whispered into his ears, "Has anyone got more birthday cake?"

Chapter Five:
The Greed of Countess Branwen

"Give me back my Rhyll!" Ned was shouting at high pitch to the huffy woman before him.

"Rhyll? What is Rhyll?" she replied, admiring the green crystals on the flat of her hand. "Can you mean my emeralds? Why these are part of my Crown Jewel Collection!"

"No, they are not! They are NOT emeralds, I know that for sure," he replied, trying to restore calm to his panicked voice.

"And you claim that they are yours? Now how could an inferior bug like you ever own something as grand as these?"

"Not own exactly. It travels with me."

She looked down a nasty nose at him, proclaiming, "Nonsense! The emeralds are mine; you will never have them!" She flounced and swooshed her flowing skirts about her, showing utter contempt at his very presence. Then she scooped up the enormous diamond that she had let drop by her feet with a free hand, comparing it side by side to the now shrieking Rhyll. "Singing emeralds!" she exclaimed. "But we will have to get you voice lessons. That is a terrible din," she observed. "Let me show you to your cell ... room, next to my Falling Star." With another skirt flourish she sniffed at Ned as she started up a set of very long stairs. "Now, what shall I call you?" she said, as she disappeared into the darkness. Ned, left below, was helpless and white-knuckled.

***

In the greenhouse that next day after his adventures with Bellflower, Sierra and the horses, Ned examined the pots he had used to plant the Rhyll. He had a theory about them. He also had something to confess to his mom.

The theory was that he had not returned to the beach on his second adventure because he had switched pots before he left. He examined this idea carefully. By the signature scratched into a fragment of the broken pot, Ned decided that this one must have been hand-made by someone perhaps living near Georgian Bay where they had bought it, or some other rustic spot in cottage country. Therefore, he reasoned, he had been taken by the Rhyll in this pot to a lake or a bay. But he expected he would never know the exact 'where' or 'when'.

So that made sense to him.

Next, he examined the pot from his latest journey. He had grabbed it so quickly at the time that he hadn't even noticed it, let alone appreciated its origins. Now he could see that it had a native Canadian feel to it. The pot looked so natural, a thin line-drawing etched into raw clay, finished in a scorched salt glaze. It showed horses chasing each other evenly around the widest part of the pot. It was so action-pact and cleverly simple, no wonder his mom had bought it.

Now that adventure made sense too.

Finally Ned came to the confession. "I broke the pot you bought last summer," he showed his Mom that lunchtime. "It was an accident; it was me being clumsy. Maybe I could get you an-other with my allowance money ... eventually ... maybe ... when I save a bit more that is?"

Mom looked at the pot, now lying in three pieces. "That isn't so bad," she determined. "With a bit of silicon glue, I could mend this, I think. Perhaps not for plants anymore," she assessed, "but it will still be a pretty pot." She winked kindly at her son.

"We could get very nice pots at the flea market this Sunday ... you know, just in case you need more?" Ned suggested, planning his next flight in his head. This was how Ned and his mother came to buy a whole job-lot of pots the next Sunday at that flea market, which Ned stored on the greenhouse shelves, ready for future adventures.

The Rhyll took its time growing, didn't return until the full moon in November. Ned was ready, though not patient. The greenhouse was more ready than he. Now in this garden building, his spaceship he called it, he stored more provisions than he had taken before. This time he filled an empty old trunk that he found in the attic crawl-space one day. In it, he packed tins of beans, peaches and spaghetti, and jars of peanut butter and strawberry jam. In the bottom, he stored three large glass jars of tap water upright, their lids sealed on tight. To this he added a tin opener, a cup, a plate, a spoon, and a kitchen knife.

Remembering the biting cold of the mountain-top, he put in mittens, a toque and a scarf. He packed tools – his trowel, of course, a hammer, nails, a screwdriver and a flashlight with extra batteries. This last item made the most sense to him because he knew he would always be travelling at night. He hid the trunk very carefully behind a stack of bags that Dad stored in a corner and seldom used.

He had yet to tell any human being about his nighttime journeys. How could he make anyone understand the excitement, about meeting mythical creatures, about doing brave things? They would think that he was imagining it all, or worse, that he had lost his mind. They would remind him that he was just an ordinary boy living in an ordinary house in an ordinary village. He could not show them his unicorn hairs, his Indigo or even his lochamour suit. They were secrets. Only Rufus knew, and he wasn't talking.

The final preparation that Ned did to the greenhouse was to fill three of his new pots, just in case. One was an oriental pot with a bamboo design; another, a blend of autumn colours swirling about bare trees; the last one, a deep blue pot, its crackle glaze dotted with white snow flakes. These he filled with soil and left on the shelves waiting, as it turned out, until that November full moon.

***

From the first minute they landed, Ned was glad he'd brought Rufus along, although there would be times when he regretted this decision. For at this very moment, what he saw outside the open door of the greenhouse got his heart pumping fast. He had barely stepped onto the plush lawn when he saw the huge fox, and a tiny fairy seconds away from its mouth. The adrenaline rush shoved him into top gear. "Look out!" he cried to the fairy as Rufus rushed at the fox sending it racing to cover in the under-growth and the fairy scuppering up into the pitch of night.

"Good boy!" he exclaimed, clapping the dog's back. He had been working on obedience training with Rufus since that last trip. It had been a struggle, turned out that they both needed training, but Ned could see how well it had paid off. Rufus stayed by his side awaiting instructions, not bouncing out of control as before. While he had a leash in his back pocket just in case, he trusted Rufus to heel on his own.

When Ned first saw the precipice his stomach flipped over. He felt a bit wonky about heights after nearly falling off that moun-tain! While it was definitely more spacious than the unicorn's back gate, it was still a really narrow and a really long precipice. He was glad that no one but Rufus noticed him sit down just then, while that jiggly feeling left his belly.

His lust for adventure was stronger than his fear of falling, however, so he soon recovered his daring. Besides this place was interesting, and not just interesting, it was fantastic! He was so far up in the mountains, higher than the moon right now! Peak after peak crowded the skyline, their many precipices nearly touching each other. Rock shelves dripped like icicles from their bottoms, while lush grasses, bushes and florals carpeted their tops. Hundreds of swing bridges made of rope and wood slats, jutting in every direction, joined them all together.

On each mountain shelf stood one huge building in a design that defied description. These structures were not like apartment buildings, nor were they like office buildings, nor anything else Ned had ever seen. It was as if you took all the houses of a village, he thought, all different in design, colour and size, and glued them all together. Each house had a roof, a porch and stairs, some made of stone, some of wood. They were stuck next to and on top of each other into a big glob of wonderful weirdness!

Splashes of light added even more intrigue to the scene, from the array of coloured lights inside each home to the spectacular green-blue waves of light dancing in the sky. *I think I read about these sky light waves*, he mused, *I think maybe these are Northern Lights. If so, I'm guessing I'm north. I used the oriental pot though. That means I'm in the east. So ...* "I must have come to the north-east world," he blurted out loud, pleased with his conclusions.

Boy and dog started exploring the cliff, leaving their supplies behind in the greenhouse for now. They walked across the well-kept grass and onto the first bridge. On the bridge they saw a man and a woman staring at each other romantically, their foreheads together, their lips just touching. Ned turned away quickly, pink-cheeked, but not before he had been seen by the couple, who shouted out and sprinted over to greet them.

"You are both so cute!" squealed the girl. "Are you a new breed of nymph?"

"Of course not!" snorted Ned, forgetting his manners. "I am a human boy," he said proudly, "This is a dog – a rather large dog actually," he added.

"We are human also," said the male of the couple, "titan-human to be precise, because we tend to be taller and stronger than regular humans." Ned had already noticed their towering height, easily two feet higher than his dad. His 'big dog' did not look any size next to them.

"My name is Ned Clery," he offered. He was finding it best on these trips to start off with a name. "This is my dog, Rufus. And please don't ask me how I came to be here because I never know how to answer that one."

"Very well. Ned ... Rufus," said the woman turning to each. "This is my spouse Elam. I am Kiri. We live in the dwelling at the end of this bridge."

Despite her great height, Kiri was delicate, with a thin face, kiss-shaped lips, narrowed green eyes, and a slender nose. Her dark blonde hair waved to shoulder length, and her otherwise pale skin was lightly freckled. She wore a slightly flared green skirt cinched tightly at the waist, with a pale cream blouse under a short mid-brown woollen jacket. In style, her clothes were simply cut, lacking adornment.

In contrast, Elam was dark and dramatic. His shaggy ebony hair matched a full beard and strong eyebrows. Deep-set brown eyes looked as if they had been placed in their sockets by sooty fingers. Plain-cut black trousers and a cable-knit sweater bulged over thick arms and legs. Were it not for his kindly expression, he would have looked quite scary.

"Have you just arrived on our scarp?" Kiri asked.

"What's a scarp?" Ned wondered aloud.

"Why this mountain ledge, this precipice as you lower-world humans call it."

"That's an easier word to remember," Ned observed, as he followed them down a set of steps and into a flower garden underneath the strange building. "Who lives in this building?" he asked. "Who lives in all of these buildings?" as he pointed a finger in every direction.

"Families, single folks, pets, plants," Elam explained. "Oh, fairies too. They find little nooks to occupy, here and there."

"Were you driven out of the lower-world for some reason, as the unicorns were?" asked Ned.

"What! No, of course not!" Kiri exclaimed. "We live here because it is the most beautiful place in all of the over-world," she pronounced proudly.

"I think that must be true," Ned agreed. "I think it might also be true that the lower-world has no idea about your over-world."

By now they were approaching the edge of the scarp, where a giant of a woman sat dangling her legs and skirts over the cliff, holding a gleaming gem in one hand. She was dressed expensively in flowing chiffon robes. Her rich chestnut hair was pulled into a tight flourishing bun, held in place by bejewelled combs. She was not beautiful as Ned knew the word, not because her face was misshapen or her nose ugly, or a wart was in the wrong place. No, she was not beautiful because she was haughty, huffing at them as they approached.

It was just then that Ned noticed the Rhyll lying on the ground by the tree under which the woman was perched. The woman must have followed his gaze to see the Rhyll moments later. Before Ned could pick it up she had dashed to it, scooped it up, and held it tightly in one huge hand.

"Thanks, that's mine. I kind of dropped it," Ned explained in his politest of voices. She turned away as if she hadn't heard, and plunked herself down on the scarp edge again.

"You'll never get it from her," Kiri whispered. "She takes everything; she never gives it back."

"But ... but that's not even possible," cried Ned in a panic. "It's not supposed to happen that way!" He tried to reason with the woman again. "Could you please give that back to me?" he asked, in his nicest manner. "You don't know how important it is." She didn't even turn, as she continued to stare at the Rhyll, holding it out over the ledge.

Only then did a desperate Ned raise his voice. "Give me back my Rhyll!" Only then did the woman turn around and bear down on him with those angry words and outrageous claims. She whisked the Rhyll away, leaving Ned in hopeless frustration.

Rufus shoved a wet nose under the limp hand of his master, nuzzling away at it. Ned was far too distracted to even notice until the dog persisted, this time with his tongue. "Sorry I got us into this mess old boy," he said quietly. "Worst thing is I have no idea how to get us out of it." His tongue felt pasty, he couldn't stop his legs from shaking, and he had to keep swallowing to stop himself from retching.

A warm arm encircled his shoulders as Kiri led him away from the edge. She guided his meek body back through the garden, under the complex of homes and up back steps to the glass foyer that marked the entrance to their place. Elam followed behind with a whimpering Rufus. Kiri led Ned to a huge chair in their simple living room. She placed a woollen blanket loosely over him for the shock. He sat there still as she prepared a warm drink, which she placed in front of him, and which he ignored.

After they had both left him in silence for a good few minutes, Elam sat down next to him. "What is so special about those emeralds Ned? Please make us understand!"

"If only it was emeralds," Ned replied, bitterness in his voice. "It isn't a gem. It is a creature from somewhere other than this world. It thinks, it talks to me," he wondered if he should say, but then he did add, " ... and it has magical powers."

"Magic eh?" Elam replied. "That is a great loss indeed. We have magic stones as well that we use everyday. Although SHE has taken most of them, we could still spare a little for you."

"You don't understand," Ned explained, the panic still within, "It brought me here – the Rhyll did – to this place and time. It kind of transported Rufus and me. I'm not really sure how it works. But I do know that without it we can't go home."

"I wish we could help you," Kiri was getting worked up herself. "THAT WOMAN!" she shouted, her fingers pointing outdoors, "She is the hardest person on all the scarps to deal with! She has stolen from us all – our jewelry, our artwork, anything of value. She has taken it all, as taxes she claims. She has them hidden in her fortress under heavy lock and key. She has stolen our heirlooms and birthrights as well and she will not give anything back! She has been banished from all the other scarps, of course, prevented from crossing their bridges. We all are stuck on this scarp with her. THAT WOMAN!"

Ned cried out in reply, "She shouldn't get away with it! She is a bully and a thief, plain and simple!" Jumping to his feet, he paced about. His brain was so scattered that he just couldn't think. She had not just stolen the Rhyll; she had kidnapped it and was holding it captive. How was he to ever forget the Rhyll's scream of protest, a horrible wail that still echoed within him? That Rhyll who had helped him to rescue others. That Rhyll who had rescued him, who needed rescuing itself now. Ned could not let it down!

Kiri and Elam watched as he tired himself out from his pacing, until he was quietly seated again. When a nervous Rufus jumped up and threw himself over his lap, Ned stroked the dog's ears fondly for a moment or two. Squeezing back tears now filling his eyes, he held the dog's head in both hands, touching their noses together, "Well at least you're here. That's a bit of home, eh boy?"

"We will give you a home for as long as you need," offered Elam, pushing the neglected drink closer to Ned. He took a deep swallow of the drink this time. It tasted a bit like tea, only sweeter with less of a bitter aftertaste; it comforted him somewhat. He stared at the couple's kind faces, "You have been good to us," he said. "As kind as you are, that's how horrible she is," he seethed, his lip curling at the thought. "I need to know more about – THAT WOMAN. I need to know my enemy, if I am to defeat her."

"Her name is Branwen," Kiri explained, "although she calls herself Countess. She is more like a tyrant than royalty. Her family were once wealthy, but that was many years ago. She thinks she is rich still, although her wealth now comes from her thefts. She thinks that she rules this scarp."

Chapter Five

"There is still one thing that I haven't told you yet," Ned sighed, "I am almost certain that while I'm here with you, your day will not dawn."

"What do you mean Ned?" Elam asked, "Of course the sun will come up, in about eight hours I would guess by the look of the sky."

Ned shook his head slowly, "I don't think so Elam. I think you'll find that it stays dark. I am sorry about that. I mean we're not supposed to stay long in any one place." Kiri and Elam looked puzzled.

"I see that you don't believe me just yet," Ned added sadly. Then attaching the leash to Rufus' collar, he started to pull him towards the door. "I think I'll go back to my greenhouse. I need to come up with a plan. I think," he yawned, "I just may need a nap. Can I come back when you see for yourselves that the day hasn't dawned?"

"Of course," they said, watching him descend their stairs to ... they were not quite sure where.

***

Ned pulled all his clothes from the trunk in the corner of the green-house and laid them out on the floor. He figured he needed a bed of sorts for Rufus and himself. He regretted not packing a sleeping bag. He spread the towel on the dusty floor and balled his scarf into a pillow. Then he put extra socks on over the ones he was wearing, placing the toque on his head. Snuggling into his coat, he sat cross-legged on the towel to think.

In fact, he never had so little thought in his head as right now. In the meanwhile, he outlined his problem...

HE was a boy, small for his age. SHE was a tall, strong woman.

HE was afraid of falling off that scarp. SHE was at home on this ledge.

HE had only tools, cutlery to defend himself. SHE probably had real weapons.

HE was in the right! SHE was in the wrong!

It was a pretty scrawny list, he thought, but it pointed clearly to something. *I can't make a plan, because I don't know enough about her*, he reasoned. *What about this fortress of hers? Where is it? What does it look like? Does she ever leave it unguarded? Where does she store all the things she has stolen? What weapons does she have? Does she have any weaknesses? What does she do all day, or all night for that matter?*

If Ned was to come up with any kind of plan he must know all this, much more. He must also understand this scarp, and the people who lived on it. With these still raw ideas fumbling about in his mind, he lay down beside Rufus and drifted into an uneasy sleep.

He awoke just a few hours later to the sound of Rufus whimpering. The dog was resting his front paws on a window sill with the view of their garden at home. Not only of their garden, his doghouse as well. "Sorry pal. That's not real, not just yet." He opened the door to let Rufus out to show him where they still were. The dog dashed out into the night, returning a minute or two later looking forlorn.

"How about breakfast?" he suggested, "Things always look better on a full stomach. That's what Dad always says." *Dad... Mom ...* He was missing them. *What if we never get home?* *Maeve...*

He shook those thoughts free for the moment and set about looking after his dog, which was dependent upon him alone. He opened a tin of beans, spooned half onto the plate, placing it on the floor for Rufus. Then he set a half-jar of water on the floor beside it, after he had taken a big swig for himself. The rest of the beans he ate cold from the tin. He was tidying up from their breakfast when he heard Kiri's voice calling his name. "Right here," he returned.

"Where Ned?" she called out. "I can only hear you."

Curious, he thought, as he stepped onto the lawn. "I was just there in my greenhouse."

"Greenhouse?"

"Yes, you know this building behind me."

"There is nothing behind you Ned," she looked confused.

Ned paused for a moment, "Oh ... Oooh. You can't see the greenhouse? Well that's interesting."

"Explain," replied Kiri, "You say a greenhouse is here?"

"Oh yes," Ned affirmed. "It must be invisible to you. I wonder if you can feel it though." He placed one of Kiri's hands lightly on the door frame.

"I do feel something, a wood texture I'm sure."

I wonder, he mused. "Would you like to come in?"

"Oh yes, if that is possible. How exciting this is," she said. "Maybe I could feel my way around."

Hmmm, maybe ... He led her over the threshold into the small glass house; she let herself be guided as if she were sightless.

"I can see it when I am inside!"

"I did wonder if you would."

Then Kiri turned around to look out the windows. "That is not my scarp!" she exclaimed. "Where am I Ned?"

"I think you're still on your scarp," he explained. "Only from these windows you are getting a view of my world. I think this is the Rhyll's way of reminding me where I have come from; where I will always want to return. See my garden just there – and there's Rufus' doghouse at the edge of the lawn. The house that I live in is just beyond in the gloom. That is where Mom and Dad will be sleeping still."

"Quite miraculous Ned! This is the work of one Rhyll?"

"I think so Kiri. That is my guess anyway, from the places we have travelled together before this."

"Amazing," she cried. "I must tell Elam." Then shifting her tone, she said solemnly, "I did come looking for you for another reason though Ned. I came to say that you were right. It is night still. Elam asks if you can please come over to our place again. We need to talk."

"Yes we do," he agreed. "I'll be along when I have exercised Rufus. It's up to me to take care of him now."

This time when a calmer Ned entered their home, he took more notice of the space. As expected, all the furnishings were of a size suited to much bigger folks. There were two comfy chairs and one well-stuffed sofa, all finished in earth-tone fabrics of coarsely-woven wool. There were simple chairs too, tables and shelving, made of natural woods. In the centre of the main room was an open fireplace, surrounded by a circular hearth. A stove pipe and hood mid-space sucked smoke from the room, although it smelled of wood smoke nonetheless. Everything was clean, pleasant and cozy, he thought. No ornaments, however, no paintings, no pictures, nothing that said who Elam and Kiri were.

This time the coffee table had been moved to a more prominent position, laden with a variety of foods. There were grainy buns and muffins in a basket, strange-looking fruits in a bowl, and a platter of interesting cheeses. A steaming pan of drink had been placed in the middle, with mugs and a ladle beside it.

But there were also people – big people – much taller than he, young and old. They sat in chairs or squatted on the floor, sharing the meal. As Ned entered the room, all eyes turned on him.

Elam made them welcome with plates of food and mugs of drink. "We have come together in a council of sorts Ned," he explained. "We are all concerned about the night, or rather the lack of a day."

"I would be myself, if I weren't so worried about the Rhyll," he said.

"We have told the others about the theft of the Rhyll, of its importance to you. We have told them what you said about the day not dawning," Kiri said, "how it is because you are here."

Chapter Five

"We want to know what you are going to do about it!" someone growled.

"What I'm going to do?" Ned asked, feeling irked by the tone of the question. "I've apologized already ... that's a start. I'll form a rescue plan, of course. I promise I won't stop 'til I've found my Rhyll."

"That is not good enough," another disgruntled voice. "We cannot live without the sun. Our crops will die and it will get unbearably cold very soon. It is your fault; it must be your solution!"

At this, Ned started to fume. "I admit that my being here is a problem," he said carefully, "but you are all to blame as well." To their shocked faces, he continued, "You have been bullied by this ... Countess, before I came. You have allowed a criminal to run free. She has taken your treasures, your memories, all that makes you special, and she has hoarded them away. Now look at you," he paused, not believing his own courage. "You sit there grumbling at an ordinary boy who you blame for all of your troubles. I will get my Rhyll back, I promise you that. But it would go faster if I had your help." He forced himself to breathe more slowly again, looking them all in the face.

"You are right of course Ned," agreed Kiri, "We have complained amongst ourselves about the Countess without trying to do anything. We are twelve in number, she is one. Why does she think she is the ruler of our scarp? She is not!"

Then Elam got up and came over to Ned. "What would you have us do?"

"We need to put our heads together," he suggested, "All ideas welcome. What about the fairies?" he asked, "Couldn't they help too?"

"Oh we do not talk to the fairies. They are like the birds. They just live wild about us."

"Then you're missing out on something very valuable," Ned proclaimed, "Some of my best friends are fairies. No, before we can plan we must have another meeting, this time with the fairies."

***

It was Ned who called the first fairy down from the tree, the one he had rescued the night before. He told her his problem, asking for her help. "Why should we help people who ignore us, who only let us have leftovers from their tables, the things that they throw away?"

"I can give you many reasons why you should," replied Ned. "For one, I saved your life. You could've been killed by that fox. And when that fox sneaked up on you, did I see you dew-watering the flowers? That must mean you're a kind of flower-fairy. Won't your flowers die without sun?" – to which the fairy nodded.

Then suspecting it was more than unicorns who couldn't resist a good story, he thought he could sweeten the pot. "I can also reward you. I've met one of your cousins – a verdi-fairy. We rescued a horse together. I will tell you about verdi-fairies, if you help us, that is." So Butterwort, as she called herself, agreed to meet with their council, and to bring some more of her kind along.

It was a strange meeting later that day – five tiny fairies, twelve giant humans, one little Ned and a dog, all crowded into Kiri and Elam's home. The titan-humans didn't even know that fairies could speak. The fairies didn't even know that titan-humans were kind. And here was a child from the lower-world quite literally stopping them in their tracks, challenging them to work together.

Elam cleared his throat to begin. "Branwen," he started, all voices hushed, "Branwen, the Countess, is THE PROBLEM ... not Ned." A mutter of agreement went through the company, Ned relaxing just a little. "What we scarp-dwellers know about the Countess is that she steals, makes fools of us all. She lives alone in her fortress on the very top of our homes where she shuts herself away during the day. When she does go out, it is only at night and she always takes the Falling Star with her. She loves to watch it glow in the dark. The Falling Star is really a diamond, the largest of our growing stones. It belongs to us all. It should be used for the growing of crops. She has no servants, no one would work for her, and so she must do everything for herself. She gets her supplies delivered at night."

"That is much more than I could have found out on my own in a month," said Ned. "But I think we can learn even more, don't you Butterwort? What do flower-fairies know?"

"Well," offered the fairy, her very first speech to larger folk, "We fairies may not come into your houses, but we do peek through your windows, walk on your roofs. We have peeked into and around Countess Branwen's home. First of all, I can tell you that she has six locks on her door for which she always carries her keys. All her deliveries are pushed through a lockable door-slot, item by item, or just left on her top step. From what we can see through her windows, she stacks her treasure in the centre of one huge room. They are pushed so tightly together that you can't really see any one thing. She doesn't even dust! Because of this mess, we haven't located your Rhyll, Ned, not from what we can see through the windows at least. Oh, one other thing," Butterwort said licking her dry nervous lips, "there is a skylight."

"A skylight?" Ned echoed. "Could we get in through there?"

"Maybe," said Butterwort, "not us fairies of course. It is screwed down tightly and it has no latch. But a good strong person with the right tools? Just maybe."

"I think I just might have the beginnings of a plan," Ned suggested, "But I need a quiet place to think it through."

"With help, Ned?" Elam suggested.

"Yes Elam. I need help from your bridge builders and weavers, I think." Elam and two others raised their hands to volunteer. "If the rest of you could just wait for us here, maybe this small group, along with Butterwort and me, could meet and come back to you soon with a plan."

So Ned brought three giant humans and one tiny fairy back to his greenhouse. When they returned two hours later, they brought with them jars of peanut butter and strawberry jam, along with a rather sneaking good plan!

***

Ned stood at the base of the long rope ladder, bracing himself to begin. The full moon was lighting their way just enough. The moment was as perfect as it ever would be. He went through the checklist in his mind once again...

The others behind him were ready to go,
their tasks well-rehearsed   – check
All the bags they would need were at hand   – check
The coil of rope was over his shoulder   – check
The fairies above them were on the look out – check
The Countess was away from home   – check
-check

Just moments before, Elam had stepped off the ladder to report, "We were able to attach the rope ladder, by standing on each other's shoulders that is. The skylight is open and pulled off to one side. It was well and truly stuck for a time. With our crow bars and your tools, that job has been done too. It is your move now Ned I think."

"Right ... Well .... Okay ..." He started up the wobbly ladder, not daring to look down as he climbed. It seemed like an hour before he finally reached the top. He stepped off the ladder and onto the roof, searching for the tie off point for his rope. Butterwort had told him about the rafters that stretched across the open hole and Ned wound one end of his rope to one of its strong planks. Then he lowered himself into the countess' secret den, as he started his rescue mission.

He had barely touched the floor when Elam whispered from above. "All set Ned. We are all in place. Watch out while I throw down the bags." He stepped back just in time to avoid the thud of heavy woollen bags beside him. As he grabbed for the booty that the Countess had thrown onto her enormous dusty pile, he barely missed a beat. He filled and tied the bags one by one, preparing them for transport.

As he would finish up with one bag he would tie it onto the rope, giving it a tug. Elam above would pull it up deftly and sling it over his shoulder to another team member just behind. The bags were then passed along the line of scarp-dwellers who took turns running them back to Ned's greenhouse. Its doorframe had been surrounded with a piece of thick yarn to clearly mark the entrance. In this way most of the stolen goods were retrieved and hidden invisible to the Countess' eyes.

He sorted and packed the mountain of treasure, looking all the while for the Rhyll. He was growing concerned as he got to the bottom and hadn't discovered it yet. Suddenly Butterwort appeared fluttering about his head, squeaking "Fly for goodness sake! Hurry Ned! The Countess returns from her walk."

Ned stopped filling the bags at once. Instead of climbing back up the rope as Elam and Butterwort urged, however, he moved further into the room. He felt along the walls for any sign of a chink that might indicate a secret hiding hole. He was going off-plan he knew, but it was only too clear to him that he should not be leaving without the Rhyll. It was not until the front door actually opened and Countess Branwen stepped in, that he was reminded of the danger he faced.

The Countess' shriek vibrated clear through his bones as something whizzed past his head. "You bug! You thief!" she cried, rushing at him. Though her arms were her only weapons at hand, she made full use of them now. "Where is my treasure?" she screamed as she knocked him down with a backhand and continued slapping her hands about in the air, connecting with him a few times more. He tried climbing the rope, but she yanked it back so hard that he tumbled to the floor again. As he fell, an object dug into his back which he grabbed onto unconsciously.

The Countess was bearing down on him once more, this time wielding an enormous sword, taking a position between him and the door. He jumped and weaved as the sword slashed the air, slipping several times in his efforts to avoid the blows. It took him a few more weaves and dives before he realized his advantage. On the next volley, as the Countess approached him again, he threw himself down on the floor, ducked under her legs, and was out the open door faster than he had ever run. She dropped the sword and pursued. While she was bigger, he was faster. He didn't stop until he had reached the greenhouse where he knew Rufus and the others were waiting, now with the yarn marking the door-frame removed. She screeched as she was foiled by the invisibility of the building, and although she paced about on the lawn just in front, she could not discover him, the treasure, or the others who were hiding within.

Eventually she gave up the search, although her wails could be heard long after she was gone from sight. It was some minutes more before Ned stopped panting enough to confess through rising sobs. "I messed up! I failed you. Worse still, I've lost the Rhyll."

Kiri rushed to his side, hugging him close to her, "No Ned, you have not failed us one bit! Look at what we have accomplished together!" she exclaimed as she pointed to all the bags stacked about them. "This is success, not failure. It is not just our memories you have given us back. We are strong now together, big and small!" Turning him to her, she looked him full in the face, "I promise we will not let your Rhyll go un-rescued. We will get it back for you yet."

Then Elam took him, wounded, in his arms and carried him back to their home. Placing him onto their bed with Rufus beside him, he tried to reassure Ned further. "Rest easy boy. Tomorrow we will make a new plan."

Ned lay back on the bed, trying to relax his aching head and bruised limbs. As Elam sat beside him, he cast his eyes down at Ned's hand. Now that Ned was relaxing his grip, Elam could see the one last thing that Ned had grabbed before his escape. "Why Ned! You have captured the Falling Star!" he gasped.

"Oh, sorry," Ned replied, "She just threw it at me. I guess this is yours." He handed Elam the great gem.

"No Ned," said Elam slowly starting to grin. "You know what this is? This is ... a new plan!"

Chapter Six:
The Peanut Butter Plan

Ned rolled the three diamonds around in his palm, as he tended to do before bed these nights. They reminded him of Elam, Kiri and Butterwort and of their fantastic homes on the scarp. Those were the good bits on which he reflected, and those were the stuff of his dreams.

He had awoken that last dark morning throbbing from the Countess' blows. A huge bump on his head shrieked still from that forceful backhand; both legs burned yet from her slaps. Despite his recent few hours of sleep, his eyes were blurry and red from a never-ending fatigue. Rufus had skipped out while he slept, but Ned no longer fretted about him. He knew now that they both were safe, no matter what the Countess might try to do next.

He had just been awake a few minutes when Kiri came in with his breakfast – thick slices of fresh bread slathered with peanut butter and jam, and a mug of that special sweet tea. "I need to get up! We're back where we started. No Rhyll and no new day." He utterly failed to pull himself off the bed, and was forced to lie back on the pillows again.

"Hush, Ned," Kiri said, "it is all in hand. Elam and some others are off to see the Countess as we speak. They should return with your Rhyll at any moment."

"H-h-how? Why would she give it back now?"

"Because of the Falling Star. She loves that above all else," Kiri explained. "She will give back the Rhyll – for the Star."

"But you said it was a great growing stone, a-a-and that you needed it for your crops."

"We may see it return to us yet. For now, we need our daylight back more. Besides, you recovered hundreds of smaller growing stones from that pile you know ... and something else ..."

She left the room for a moment and returned clasping onto a framed painting, which she showed to him now. "This is my mother," she said softly. "I have not seen her face for many years. You recovered this portrait from the Countess' lair. To me, this is more precious than anything."

Butterwort buzzed into the room at this very moment and threw herself onto the bed. "You look very bad Ned," she pronounced, "those bruises are going to go black and then purple and then yellow and then..."

"Hold on cheeky fairy," laughed Ned, "you're as bad as your cousin."

"Ah, that is what I have come for – the story you promised."

Kiri left them to talk while she sorted through bags, to return everything to its rightful owner, with better locks on their doors this time. Before Ned even began his story, however, he opened the tiny pouch from the lace around his neck, retrieved a unicorn hair which he broke in two, floating one half in his tea, returning the rest to the pouch.

"What is that?" she asked with a flutter of wings.

"Secrets," Ned replied, holding a finger to his lips. He did tell her about Bellflower, however, and about their adventures that night – except for the whereabouts of unicorns. Butterwort bounced up and down on the blankets at the sauciness of Bellflower, flew about the room at the thought of other winged creatures, and cried happy tears at the success of the medicine for Tansy the mare. As he spoke, the unicorn's hair worked its magic so quickly that his bruises were little more than a memory, even before he had finished his tale.

By then Elam had returned with a very grim-looking Rhyll. Ned and Kiri, working quickly, were able to restore its gleam with good soil, fresh water and one growing stone.

Now each time he looked at those tiny bright stones, Ned remembered his bittersweet leaving – the back slaps all around, the ear-tweaks from Butterwort, the smothering hugs from Elam and Kiri. Then those final few seconds, when before shutting the door to the greenhouse, he felt Kiri's hand reach out searching for one of his own, pressing two more growing stones into his palm, and folding his fingers around them.

***

Now that he understood more of the rules, Ned no longer waited by the window at night. He posted a calendar instead which showed the dates and phases of the moon. He only watched out on nights when it was at its fullest. Not that he expected to see his Rhyll in all this snow. Not that he expected to see the Rhyll at all!

By late December snow was lying two feet deep on the hills, ice had thickened the ponds. Ned and Maeve squeezed all the fun they could from this season, tobogganing down those very hills and skating on those same ponds. He learned to skate that year. He just had to after Maeve double-dared him. She taught him with patience and a great deal of squealing, as he grabbed onto her to steady himself, until he was able to go it alone. With her tutoring and long hours of practice he became a fair skater, not great enough for a hockey league yet but good enough to play on Island Lake with Maeve and a few of her friends in the January deep-freeze.

One dull morning in February that year Ned awoke with a start, "Hold on, why did I never think of this before? That Rhyll could have gotten away from the Countess! It can travel anywhere using its magic, so why wouldn't it have just escaped? I mean, if it wasn't helpless, why did it stay in that smelly old place? Why did I have to rescue it?" He was getting better at working out the where, when and how of his adventures but knew he was just as hopeless about why.

When the ground had warmed up, the risk of frost being over, Ned planted his garden. This time along with his selection of seeds he sowed two growing stones into the soil, keeping back one for the pot. His plants looked quite strong by the June full moon when his next adventure began.

***

It seemed that Ned and Rufus had come to the edge of a forest this time. Inside its scary darkness, hundreds of evergreens – pines, firs, junipers – huddled together like mobsters. Was it even possible to push into their dense screen? Neither Ned nor Rufus were tempted to try, certainly not in the night, never on their own. Just west of this black thickness was a clearing of sorts with large well-spaced, bare-branched maples and oaks. The openness of the space allowed wild grasses and ferns to grow which glistened damply in the ghostly light of an orange moon. At the base of each tree, fallen leaves of orange, brown, red and yellow slowly shrivelled; flowers drooped their heads. From such clues Ned reckoned that it must early autumn of some year or other.

In one gnarly old maple with wide-reaching branches a wooden tree-house was nesting. Large enough to hold a small family, it was two storeys in height with two entrances. A full set of wooden stairs climbed to its front door, a ladder leaned against its open deck. The silver-grey siding with moss-covered roof made it hard to distinguish from the tree itself.

Ned's explorations were briefly interrupted by the Rhyll directly blocking his path. "Aha," he softly commented, reaching to scoop it into his knapsack, "I suppose you don't mean me to chase you this time? Does the journey start here?"

A hum and a glow.

He looked about even more scrupulously now. It was then that he noticed, a short distance away, a man and a boy standing all shimmery in the moon's full orb. By their appearance, he was certain that he was about to meet magic again, because, while they were the height of normal folks, that is to say that the man was as tall as Ned's dad, they were so very thin, their skin was mottled-grey, their heads completely hairless. Their clothing, which fitted like gymnasts' costumes, was grey-toned as well.

Rufus sat obediently as Ned prepared his greeting. He had only just cleared his throat, not even uttered a word, when man and boy vanished clean from sight. "Oh? Oh no! ... What? ... Where?" a flummoxed Ned sputtered. *They must still be around*, he thought, *no one and nothing moves that fast*. He whispered into the gloom, "My name is Ned Clery. I am a human, nearly twelve-year-old boy. This shaggy thing with me is my dog Rufus. We have just come to visit ... A-a-and neither of us is scary."

Then they sat down waiting in the dewy wild grass until their bottoms began to feel uncomfortably moist. This prompted Ned to try a different approach. He commanded Rufus to stay in place, got to his feet and returned to the greenhouse. There he packed a few more items into his knapsack before making his way back to the clearing. He pulled out his coarse-woven blanket (another gift from Kiri), spread it on the ground and began to lay out a picnic. He made three peanut butter and jam sandwiches, using some of his provisions, along with fresh bread he'd put in at the last minute. Then he arranged them on his only plate after cutting them all in two. For Rufus he opened a tin of cold spaghetti which he placed to one side of the blanket. When his table had been set and the picnic laid out he took up a half-sandwich and started to eat. "There's enough for everyone," he called out.

As Ned chewed away at his sandwich, he continued to watch all the while. He was just pushing one last bite into his mouth when he thought he spied movement by the base of the tree. A full minute more, man and boy stepped into the open and Ned saw them at last. He held his breath as they dared to come closer; stayed motionless while they sat on the blanket picking up a half-sandwich each. His muscles had begun to cramp from his statue-like freeze as he waited while they nibbled their treats. Only when he was sure they were enjoying his food did he allow himself a brief comment, "Good huh?"

The man wiped his lips with one wrist, smacking the last of the peanut butter around in his mouth, before he spoke. "May I take one ... for my wife?"

"Take the rest please. I have lots left." Ned waited while the man climbed the steps to the tree-house taking the boy along with him.

A full fifteen minutes passed before the door to the house opened and the man emerged alone. This time he walked straight up to where young Ned was seated. "Good food. What is it called?"

"Well, this jar is peanut butter and this one is strawberry jam," Ned explained.

"Ah," said the man. "We have strawberries. But 'peanut butter'.... it is miraculous!"

"I have more," Ned said feeling pleased with himself, "One more jar in my greenhouse ... plenty at home."

"Where is 'home'?"

"Ah, that's a good question," he replied, "I don't have a really good answer, of course."

"My home is this tree. My family – my wife and son wait," he said gesturing in the direction of the tree. It took Ned a minute or two to realize that this had been an invitation from the grey man, and that he and Rufus were expected to follow him up to his strange but wonderful home.

What struck him most obviously about the inside of the tree-house was its total lack of colour. Everything seemed to be in tones of grey with just a bit of moss green here and there. The only source of light in the room came from the many candles flickering in elaborate wooden candlesticks. In the eating area were two wooden benches which fitted snugly beneath one single table. A large low-slung bed pushed against one wall seemed to serve as a sofa as well. The kitchen was compact with open shelves on which were displayed a few pieces of cutlery, plates, cups, and bowls; one cupboard storing their food. A pot-bellied stove on which the woman was preparing a meal served the additional function of heating the space. A narrow twig ladder led to the second floor, a half-floor, one smaller bed just visible along the open edge.

But what really excited Ned were the many woodcarvings that landscaped the room on every surface – on the walls, on bedposts, on the cupboard, shelves, benches and table. They were heavily detailed, life-like, and all whittled from a natural silvery wood. There were shelves of carvings which stood on their own bases, mostly of forest creatures, such as bears, wolves, squirrels, and chipmunks. Each piece of furniture had been detailed in relief designs with birds such as owls, ravens, and crows; also flowers, trees, and ferns.

Ned was stopped in his tracks by the look of the walls. He was reminded of the lochamour cavern with its mosaics, tapestries and paintings. These carved wooden panels were telling tales as well. The lore they seemed to be telling concerned long thin human-like characters all looking very much like the man, woman and child who stood before him.

Unlike the man and the boy, the woman had hair – beautiful, straight, shoulder-length grey hair. She was also grey head to toe, young, elegant, and thin except for a bulging mid-drift area which meant she was soon going to have a baby. *But a baby what*? Ned wondered. *Who are these folks*? *What are they*?

The woman gestured to Ned to take a seat at the table, placing a plate of stew in front of him as he sat. Although the meat was something he could not recognize, some of the berries it was cooked in looked familiar. There were raspberries, blackberries, blueberries, along with tiny leaves that he couldn't name. It would have been impolite not to taste their food especially as they had tried his. Ned dipped a spoon into the mixture and touched it to his tongue. The sweet berries and tangy herbs mingled with the saltiness of the meat reminded Ned of mincemeat pies that his mom would make at Christmas. He had no trouble at all finishing this fruity stew off, and scraping the plate clean afterwards.

Throughout the entire meal, not a word had been spoken. In fact these folks seemed to be quite comfortable with the silence. But Ned was not. When he could stand it no longer, he filled the silence himself. He told them in brief about his village; about the old house where he lived with his parents; about his dad's great garden and his little piece of it. He described his best friend Maeve, all the fun they had together. He even talked about his school, his favourite subjects – science, art and literature. He did not mention magic. Then when he felt sure he had chattered enough, he sat silent and waited.

When she finally did speak Ned found the woman's voice quite soothing, like wind rustling through trees. "I am called Betula. Laurus is my spouse. This is Rhus, our son. We will have another child soon. We are not human as you are; we are sylvan."

"I've never met sylvans before," Ned observed, "Fairies of course but not sylvans. Are you nymphal like fairies or mermaids?"

This time it was Laurus who responded, "Not nymphal, no. We are elvish. We are the wood elves who take care of the forests. We water the trees in droughts when water is scarce; we scatter seeds evenly to reforest; we tend to them when they are ill with funguses or parasites. It is true that we also use their wood for our homes, and for the carvings that we use to barter for what we cannot find for ourselves. But we only take as much as we need to survive and we take fallen wood first."

As Laurus spoke, Ned's eyes travelled to a particular panel on the wall. "This tells about how you look after the trees, doesn't it?"

he observed. Then moving along to the next one he said, "Here on this panel where a sylvan is holding a bow, another is holding a spear? ..."

"Ah, yes. We do take what meat we need, but we do not kill for pleasure."

"This one?" asked Ned, "What does this one say?"

"It is the story of the great fire that destroyed all our forests many years ago."

"I think I know that story," Ned replied. "I know some nymphal creatures whose wings were singed off after an asteroid struck the earth. They took to the water to survive."

"During that bad time also, the wood elves dug deep beneath the trees and waited out the heat and flames underground. When the forest re-grew after the long, deep winter some of us returned to the surface while others remained beneath."

"Like the root people?" young Rhus spoke up.

"Exactly, like the root *elves*," Laurus corrected, smiling kindly at his son.

"Root elves?" asked the ever-curious Ned.

"We can show you far better than we can tell you," offered Betula, beckoning Ned and Rufus to follow.

The sylvans led their visitors to the exact same spot where Ned had found his Rhyll, when he and Rufus first landed. *It must be telling me something*, mused Ned, his curiosity increasing even further.

Little Rhus took a stick and scratched away at the area until the outline of a small hatch appeared in the ground. "Here it is!" he exclaimed.

"This is one of many doors to the under-trees," Laurus explained. "An elderly root couple reside below; have done so since long before we came. She is called Linden, he is Racine. In the prime of their lives they were the tunnel-builders of this forest, helping to scrape out underground homes for creatures such as moles, field mice, foxes, rabbits. It is an ancient art-form, sadly one that may be lost forever. Nowadays the children of the root elves have abandoned them in favour of the upper trees, even of the outer world at large," Laurus added with a shiver.

"Maybe I'll call on root elves," Ned suggested. He was still puzzling together why the Rhyll had chosen this doorway and he was itching to find out. "Are you coming you too?"

"Oh no!" Laurus nervously replied. "We never go down to the roots."

"Why not?" he asked. "Are they nasty or scary?"

"No, the root elves are quiet neighbours that give us no trouble," Betula mused, "It is just that it is no longer our custom to travel under-tree."

"'Time to change a custom when it doesn't make sense', my Gran always says," Ned replied. Pulling the hatch open he peered into the deep hole. But it was so pitch that he stopped before entering, "Hold on just a minute. This might be the perfect time for a flashlight."

By the time he'd returned from the greenhouse, Laurus was waiting at the entrance with a flaming torch of his own. "We have given thought to your words Ned. We think you might be right. What reason can we have not to go under-tree, especially when a young boy ventures there?"

So Ned, Laurus and Rufus braved the inky depths, shining their lights along the rough sloping tunnel until they came to some well-constructed steps which took them deep below. The west turn at the bottom of the steps was effectively blocked by a tangle of roots, while the east passage looked quite open. So, east seemed the sensible choice. As they pushed forward they called out, but nothing stirred in the dimness ahead. "Perhaps they're gone," observed Ned, "but then again ... maybe something's wrong."

Something was wrong of course. They could smell it – a sickening pervasive stench hanging thickly in the air. Even in the few minutes they'd been under-tree, they were beginning to feel nauseated. "More speed, less caution Ned," Laurus advised as they came to an open cavern.

To call the space where they found themselves 'spooky' only just began to describe it. A room had been roughed out with uneven stucco walls. Bats hung like chandeliers from the root-infested ceiling. The chamber was barely lit by minute fireflies flashing randomly throughout. There was furniture, but only a little. At the far end, a twig bed swung by the roots from above. Placed mid-room were a rustic table and chair at which a craggy female elf sat in a daze. Slumped on the floor at her feet an elderly male elf languished.

Given the overpowering, possibly poisonous, scent throughout, it was no wonder these root elves were limp. Ned turned to Laurus trying not to let the panic in his voice show. "We need to get these elves out of here, now! They might be dying in this rotting place." Laurus grabbed for the unconscious elf-woman and half-carried, half-dragged her up the stairs, while Ned stayed with the elf-man until Laurus could return to bring him to safety as well. Once topside they took in great gulps of fresh air trying to expel the horrid fumes from their lungs and noses.

Ned grabbed at the hatch-door to re-seal the condemned hole, but before he had locked it down, he was stopped short by the faint, but all too familiar, noise coming through the tunnel opening – the sound of a barking dog. Rufus had stayed below! He raced back down the steps finding the dog howling furiously into the tangle of roots. The dog's call was being answered by a wailing from within. Some creature was there!

Without giving it much thought at all, Ned locked a leash onto Rufus' collar, tying him to the steps with a firm 'sit' and 'stay'. Then placing the Indigo under his tongue to allow him to hold his breath, Ned began to crawl through the foul snarl of dirty bramble. His flashlight proved almost ineffective in this thicket; he was forced to rely more on his ears to direct him that short distance towards the moaning. In just a few minutes he had discovered the location of the creature, the source of both the haunting noises and the wicked stench which surrounded it in a nasty green fog.

He rested on his haunches out of the way as the creature hungrily gnawed away at a heavy tree root. In this sooty darkness he could see little detail. But the narrow beam of his flashlight did pinpoint a long furry body in tones of brown, and about the size of Rufus. Its face was sadly sweet, but also sinister he thought, a white snout and a black mask about the eyes which glowed vivid yellow in the artificial glare. At his approach the moans turned to snarls and the sweetness of the face instantly turned nasty, and toothy, as it snapped at the air. Ned backed away as quickly as he could without getting caught up in the mess. Then he hid under a root until the snarls turned to moans again, at which point he re-traced his route by homing in on Rufus' howls.

By the time Ned and Rufus returned to the surface, Laurus had taken the old elves up to his home and Betula had begun to care for their needs. The old folks were resting together on the bed-sofa, blankets wrapped around their frail bodies. Ned and Rufus slipped back into the room quietly and sat at the table out of the way, Ned deep in thought. In the candlelight he could make out the features of the couple. Although they looked like the syl-vans in many ways, there were differences too. While the sylvans were mainly grey-toned, these root-elves were brown all over. Their skin was rough and craggy like the bark of old trees. If their brown tattered clothes had fit at one time, they certainly hung loosely now. They were dirty and very smelly.

Watching over them as they napped fitfully, Ned became so unbearably sad that Betula sat down next to him placing her hand over his. "I am thinking of my own grandparents," he mumbled, "how I can't wait to see them again." Then to Laurus, he asked, "What do you suppose Rufus was barking at in the roots of the tree?"

"It is a stink," a gravelling voice spoke out from the bed. The old elf raised himself on one elbow, "... an evil-smelling, wicked creature. It has ruined our home. And, it wants to eat us as well! Only today it tried to enter our home as we slept!" Then the old fellow lay back gasping for breath again.

Ned whispered to Betula, "Do you think that tea would help them?" With her permission, he prepared the hot drink while Betula heated up leftover stew. Before he placed the teapot onto the tray, however, he secretly slipped half a unicorn hair under the pot's lid. Then he took both food and drink to these strange guests. He was pleased to watch them revive before his eyes.

"Can you tell me more about this stink, Grandpa Racine?" he urged, when the old man was sitting up again, looking much improved.

"We cannot and dare not get close enough to see what it is," said Racine, "But I have heard tell about such creatures before. Just how long it has been in the nether regions around our homeland is anyone's guess. For a time we barely noticed it, and because we are used to sharing the under-roots region with all manner of creatures, we did not mind. But then about two new moons ago the creature began to moan. These moans turned to howls, the howls to the foulest of odours. Now the plague of it invades every cranny of our lives and has nearly robbed us of our sanity."

"I think your stink is a wolverine," Ned observed calmly, "It is pretty vicious with long yellow fangs, but I think it is more lonely and hungry than evil. It wants to eat something, but I don't think it's elf that it wants."

"You have seen this creature Ned? How? When?" Laurus moved over and sat next to him.

"It was Rufus who found it first. Then I kind of ... snuck up on it."

"But the air in there is so poisonous!" Laurus observed, "How could you have gotten close enough to see?"

"I'm pretty good at holding my breath," he said vaguely, moving off this explanation quickly.

"How do you know what it is?"

"It looks like the wolverines I saw at the zoo last year with my science class. Mr. Evans my teacher said that they are also called stink bears. So if you know it as a stink that would make sense wouldn't it?"

"And how do you know it does not wish us harm?" asked Racine, the grudge still apparent in his tone.

"Wolverines are the fierce enemy of many animals Grandpa Racine. They're one of the toughest creatures for their size. But this one looked more scared than mad. It got angry when I came too close of course, but that's instinct. Making that awful smell is instinct too, and we all wish they wouldn't do it. You say it has been stuck in there for a long time. From what I could see, its only food has been bugs and roots. I think it must be hungry, lonely ... and maybe even lost."

"It cannot stay there," Racine exclaimed. "We need to get rid!"

"Yes, well ..." mumbled Ned, his mind drifting off into planning mode. He got so deep into his own thoughts, so immersed in solving the puzzle, that he ignored all sorts that usually delighted him on his travels to mythical places. He didn't hear Betula whistling like a soft breeze as she prepared the sourdough starter for her early morning bread-making. He missed watching Rufus play with the elf-child who was throwing acorns, shrieking as the dog caught them in his mouth and spit them out again. Most importantly, as it turned out, he failed to observe how Laurus seemed to be communicating with the older elves without the use of speech. All these wonders he ignored, as he mulled and searched his nearly twelve-year-old brain. When he finally did emerge from his thoughts, he had a headful of questions instead.

"Do you know where stinks live Grandpa Racine?"

"Never want to."

Maybe the Rhyll could ... he thought to himself. What he didn't know at this point, but what he might have figured out if he had only been watching the elves more carefully, was that they could communicate in thought; that the reason for their long silences was that they were not dependent on mere words. They only spoke out in the presence of humans, who as a rule are not gifted in this way.

"Did you say *Rhyll*, lad?" asked Racine, rising to his feet to join him at the table. "Do you know a Rhyll?"

After his problem with the Countess, Ned had determined to be far more secretive about the Rhyll. For this reason alone he was certain he had not said "Rhyll" out loud. "No, I *thought* Rhyll," he retorted, "I ... I didn't *say* it!"

"No matter, that is what I heard. Can I see it?" asked Racine. When Ned hesitated he added, "I've seen one before you understand." Ned looked up in interest. "I saw one, about a hundred and twenty years ago it was, one that befriended my father. Rhylls are very particular who they take as friends you know. Only the most special they say."

He lifted his knapsack off the floor, placed it on the table and opened its flap. All the elves crowded around wide-eyed. At this reveal the Rhyll became active, flashing a couple of brilliant glows and humming tunefully. Addressing Racine specifically, Ned said, "I know it understands me ... but I don't understand it quite yet."

"Hmmm, let me think," Racine muttered, taking the potted Rhyll from the bag and placing it in full view on the table. "It was a while back, but I think I can remember at least part of what Father told me. I think I remember him saying – I was just a young lad you understand ..."

"Yes ...." They were all leaning forward, waiting on what Racine would say next.

Racine smiled then went on. "Rhylls come from another galaxy. I can't say closer than that. They travelled here as tiny spores, oh centuries ago it was. Anyway when they got here they burrowed under the earth into empty air pockets, which was the best environment for them with its underground streams. They chose caverns smaller than the ones we live in ourselves, tiny caves where tree mites live."

"Tree mites?" prompted Ned.

"Sure, they look like tiny elves. I don't know what they used to do before the Rhyll spores arrived, but after they discovered what the spores were, the tree mites became Rhyll-herds. They cared for them from spore-infancy to the size of this one and bigger."

"How did the tree mites learn about Rhylls?" Ned asked, "Did they learn each other's language?"

"Rhylls seem to understand any language of earth almost right away."

"I know," Ned replied, "but it only glows and hums."

"Oh more than that lad," Racine added. "As I remember my father saying, his gave him visions."

"What? How Grandpa Racine?" Ned was on his feet.

"It is something about how you touch them," said Racine, "or rather where." He placed his face up close to the Rhyll, squinting his worn-out eyes to focus better.

"I-I-I've touched it, and I've carried it around quite a bit," Ned replied, "but it hasn't talked to me yet, at least nothing more than a glow ... or a hum."

"Ah, but how did you touch it, and where? I don't think it is the caps, stems or roots that you touch. What was that place? ..." Cocking his head to look at the Rhyll's profile, Racine's eyes suddenly lit up, "I think I remember. I think it is these ruffles under the cap that are its vision-chords. I am almost sure ... Anyway a true friend would be able to test this out."

Ned moved his chair closer to the Rhyll. "Is that right? Am I a true friend?" he asked it. A hum and a glow; a glow and a hum. "That's a yes!" he announced to his elvish friends with a laugh. With all fingertips of both hands he touched the ruffly undersurface of the largest cap. His expression changed from uncertainty to absolute wonder. He stayed in this position for a full fifteen minutes. Then dropping his hands slowly, and rubbing his palms over his knees, he announced in a strange, soft voice, "I think I know exactly what to do about the stink Grandpa Racine. I think I know a few other things besides."

***

Ned looked up at Laurus who was hammering a last nail into the wooden frame of the twiggy cage. "Do you think this will hold Laurus?" he asked.

"I think it looks very strong Ned. It would hold a creature as big as a bear. But I still do not understand how we get the stink from that poisonous tangle into this cage."

"The same way I got you to like me," Ned said, picking up his few tools and placing them back in his knapsack. When they were back in the tree-house he made up some more peanut butter sandwiches to which he added another half unicorn hair. He cut the sandwiches into tiny pieces and placed them in a small flower pot which he tucked into his jacket. Then, leaving Rufus in the care of the other sylvans, Ned and Laurus returned to the hatch.

He insisted on entering the tunnel alone, knowing it was a one-person job on this occasion, to fetch the creature from the nether regions of the under-root, a place he hoped to be visiting for the very last time. With the Indigo under-tongue he found the spot where he had discovered the stink two hours before, more confident this time of his path.

The animal had not moved since his last visit and it looked just as forlorn. The snarls rose again as soon as it sensed him near and this time it swiped with its claws too. Ned had taken the chair from the root-elves' home to hold it back as a lion-trainer would do to tame a beast. Keeping the chair between him and the wolverine, he crept forward as closely as he dared before tossing in the first peanut butter treat. Within moments the stink's nose was up in the air sniffing out this added aroma, which must have been quite the challenge to do over its own noxious scent. Then it crept closer, snuffled, licked once and gobbled it up, routing about for more.

In this way, he enticed the creature forward tossing bits in front of his chair shield every few feet. He and the stink moved slowly together through the root system, up the stairs and into the fresh night air. As he emerged, drawing the morose stink in his wake, Laurus was at the ready. No sooner had the animal entered the cage in pursuit of six more peanut butter pieces than Laurus deftly shut the cage door.

Once the animal was secured, Ned leaned up against a tree and wiped away the sweat that dotted his entire body. Only in hindsight did he realize what a crazy thing he had done. But once he calmed down, the sweat starting to dry, he looked again at the caged creature and feelings of pity replaced his fear. "I feel bad tricking it like that. I knew someone once that was trapped by a cage," he confessed to Laurus sadly.

"It will not be for long Ned. Let us remember that our intent is kind, for both the stink and the root-elves." They returned once again to the tree-house, leaving a rather discontented stink caged and snarling in the chilly air.

"Although I am new to Rhyll language," Ned explained to the roomful of elves, "I think I got an image of the stink's home. Its den is a cave halfway up a rocky hill. There are a lot of trees far off to one side which lead downhill to the forest's edge. At the bottom of the hill on the other side there's a low stone wall, and beyond this I'm not sure ..."

"That is not quite enough to go on lad. I cannot think of any place by our forest that looks like what you describe. Think of more ... please?" Racine urged him kindly.

Ned closed his eyes tighter. "Beyond this? ... Yes, there are yellow flowers at the bottom of the hill on the other side of the wall. Not just a small number, a lot of them, a big yellow field."

"Ah," exclaimed Betula, "when you mention flowers Ned I know just who to consult. She opened the door and stood on the balcony whistling in her breezy way. Within two minutes a fairy dropped from the sky and nuzzled next to her ear. They remained in this pose for a minute or more before Betula returned to the room, the fairy in place on her shoulder.

"This is Poppy," she explained, "a very old friend. She knows where the yellow field is."

"Excited to meet you," Ned greeted her with great enthusiasm, "I know a few cousins of yours. My name's Ned Clery."

"Ned Clery is it?" Poppy said, "I have heard about you through flower-fairy lore."

"Really!" Ned exclaimed, "I am the subject of flower-fairy tales? How wonderful! What did they say?"

"They say, 'he is mostly helpful, but can be quite rude at times'," Poppy replied.

"Ha-ha!" giggled Ned, "Not a bad reputation when you remember that most fairies are rude too!"

"So," said Poppy, "you want to get to *Quickhatch Roost* over the alpine meadows do you? Nothing could be easier!"

"But that is beyond the forest boundaries," complained Racine, "It has never been our custom to travel beyond our trees, certainly not as far as the hills."

Ned patted one of Racine's gnarly old hands with one of his own small pink ones, and repeated what he had said earlier to Laurus. "'Time to change a custom when it doesn't make sense' my Gran always says."

***

There were a few things that Ned couldn't abide about their trip beyond the edge of the woods that night, pushing a wheelbarrow full of caged stink. He hated the conifer needles thrashing at him and leaving red welts on his skin as he pushed past the tightly packed trees. He shuddered to remember the inky blackness that his eyes could not adjust to. But what Ned liked least of all was the sadness in the eyes, the mournful cries mixed with snarls, of a stink that could not understand the confines of its cage; who moaned continuously, despite all the peanut butter bits he could shove at it.

What Ned quite liked about their forest journey was having a fairy on his shoulder chattering into his ear the whole time. He enjoyed the old elf and the young one working together, pushing and pulling that wheelbarrow, dodging the occasional paw that swiped at them through the bars. It was a great relief at their journey's end, as they waded through the buttercup meadow and lifted the cage over the low stone wall, to release the stink from the cage. But what Ned liked most of all were the tears streaming down Racine's roughened face as he watched the wolverine, that stink bear he'd hated and feared, leave the cage, scupper up the hill as far as an outcropping of rocks, and lick the tip of another snout pushing out from a blackened hollow within the hillside.

They returned to a surprisingly ordered tree-house. As he entered, Betula ran to Ned with a giggle, "Just look at what Rhyll-soaked water can do Ned! What a brilliant lad you are!"

"It was the Rhyll's idea, to be truthful," he confessed. "It showed me what to do."

"We have washed all the clothes and bedding," she described, "in both our home and in the root dwelling. We have bathed ourselves, Rufus and Rhus as well. We all smell sweet. But best of all uses we made of Rhyll water was placing some into a boiling kettle so that its vapours could remove the stench from the air. This we have done in the upper-tree and in all areas of the under-tree as well.

Racine crossed, open-mouthed, to his spouse Linden who not only looked clean but twenty years younger after her Rhyll treatment. "Who is this young girl I am seeing here?" he asked in wonder, "I used to know her!"

"But that dirty old root-elf needs a good scrubbing," she laughed. "So do you all!"

***

"I'll leave you with more Rhyll water then," said Ned as he packed himself, Rufus and the Rhyll up to leave, "This jar of peanut butter besides."

"Must you leave so soon?" Betula asked. "Rhus will be so sad when he wakes."

"Yes you must," said Racine knowingly, "You do need to go right now don't you Ned?"

"Yes ... I do. I always seem to have to leave the party," he said, "just as I'm starting to really enjoy myself."

Laurus walked with Ned part of the way along his return path. "I have so many questions that don't get answered on my adventures," Ned told him. "But this one really niggles at my brain. Just how did you and little Rhus disappear when I first saw you there on that rise?"

"I suppose you deserve to know that trick Ned," he replied. Then placing one of his tiny carvings – that of a chipmunk – into Ned's hands as his parting present, Laurus walked over to the nearest tree, smiled, waved, turned his back – and disappeared.

Ned chuckled.

Chapter Seven:
The Legend of Finn the Lighthouse Keeper

Ned sat morosely in a very dense fog pulling Rufus in closer. He could hear the waves slapping against rocks. At this moment he had to confess he was seriously miffed with the Rhyll. After all, at this full moon night in a very cold March at home, he had planned for a swim at a warm beach for his next adventure, maybe a visit to the lochamours again. He did not expect a rough cliff at a wild ocean cove!

He had even made the pot for the Rhyll himself this time, since he accidentally broke the one they had used to visit the lochamours before. Or maybe not made it precisely, but he had decorated a terracotta pot with all the tiny shells he had been collecting for five years, from his visits to lake shores and ocean fronts on holidays with his parents. He had even sacrificed his most precious seashell, the one he had found on Cape Breton Island this past summer.

So why was he stuck on the cold rock-surface, in mist as thick as soup, the boom of a fog-horn shaking his brain, a wet dog at his side?

***

In the October following his twelfth birthday Ned was as glad as ever to find the Rhyll in his garden again. He had harvested all his vegetables, had spread straw on the ground, mixed with the fallen leaves, to enrich the soil and protect it over winter. The evening of that full moon was perfect. It had been a cool October, but the past few days had been warm, Indian Summer Dad had called it, like an echo of the hot days they had just been through.

Ned had decided that he wanted it be just him and the Rhyll this time. He wanted to learn its language, to understand it better. He wished to learn its stories, its own travels in the only way he could know, on a journey through its vision-chords. That warm clear October night in his garden was ideal for an adventure of this sort. To his delight he realized that he could not only see, but he could also hear the vibrations of the Rhyll's memories. He knew right away that these images were not scenes of his planet. "This is your home world isn't it?" What Ned saw was a landscape of vapours, coloured layers of vapours in fact. Rhylls floated on ribbons through these gases following them along to icy islands. They floated towards frozen landscapes cloistering into various patterns, each exquisitely distinct. Every cluster had its own vibration; Ned listened intently to the intricate harmonic blends. It all seemed impossible, but so very peaceful as well. He could sit there for days he knew, watching, listening.

Then the images became very blurred and ceased. "Something happened?" he asked the dread apparent in his voice. Another vision – this time of a dark sun and a dull ruined world. A vision of spores flying through endless space whizzing aimlessly past planets, through galaxies. Then a slowing down, a hovering, a moving into orbit around a blue-green planet marbled with wisps of white.

"That's my planet isn't it?" he observed. "That's why you've come." Taking his fingers away, he whimpered, "I'm so ... sorry." He stayed by the Rhyll's side all that night in sympathetic vigil until as he had come to expect, just before dawn, the Rhyll vanished into the ground.

***

So it was more than a little odd at this time that Ned had forgotten his compassion for the Rhyll. But at this very moment, as he sat marooned in the fog on a rock far away from his home not knowing in which direction to move, Ned was … miffed.

"I think the trick here Rufus is not to panic. I did for a second there ... I'm past it now. No good going back into the greenhouse because we have to find the Rhyll. I-I'm sure this fog will roll off soon." All this was said to comfort the dog, while the master remained in dismay.

It was just then that they both heard carrying over the misty bleakness – a sound, a deep voice, a singing voice, alone, echoing...

When he were a lad of ten, Finn asked his Ma',
"Can I go off to the sea?"
"No lad you are young to go seafaring,
You must remain with me."

When Finn were thirteen, he asked his Da'
"Can I go off to the sea?"
"No lad you are young to go seafaring,
You must remain with me."

"You're a fool," they said, "but a brave one.
It's never be done before.
Rest your oars, tie your boat, come with us,
Or you'll never return to shore."

When Finn were sixteen he asked his Ma',
"Can I go off to the sea?"
"Young man you are ready for seafaring,
Though I wish you would stay with me."

Chapter Seven

At seventeen years, his captain said,
"Finn, fix those sails for me.
Young man you are built for seafaring
Much more than the likes of me."

"You're a fool," they said, "but a brave one.
It's never be done before.
Rest your oars, tie your boat, come with us,
Or you'll never return to shore."

"Finn were twenty one when the ship went in
Throwin' him into the sea,
But he came out safe though his mates were drowned,
"And they never returned to me."

At thirty years old he came to his wife,
"I will go again to the sea.
There are thirteen souls for the saving,
I must!" "No, stay with me!"

"You're a fool," they said, "but a brave one.
It's never be done before.
Rest your oars, tie your boat, come with us,
Or you'll never return to shore."

He were thirty years old when he saved the ten,
And returned for three more in the sea.
Finn lost his own soul a'searching,
And he never returned to me.

"You're a fool," they said, "but a brave one.
It's never be done before.
Rest your oars, tie your boat, come with us."
... and he never returned to shore.

***

Ned and Rufus followed all the verses and choruses until, just as the last strains of it ended, they had come upon the source. "Sad song," Ned whispered, coming closer to an elderly singer seated on the edge of a cliff overlooking a foggy, narrow straight of water.

"Yup" said the singer. He was an old man with a wrinkled face and a sparse beard, not too tall, though definitely human. *No magic there*, Ned thought to himself. He was the image of an old salt in Ned's mind – a sailor's cap, denim overalls, a rather grubby jersey, all of which had seen better days. On his feet he wore rubber Wellingtons with a few frayed threads of lining peering over their tops.

"Did you know that man, the man in the song ... Finn?" Ned asked.

"Nope," said the man, "He were me Grandpa, still and all."

Ned pulled Rufus down beside him and sat on the rock a short distance from the man, "I guess something bad happened to him?"

"Yup," said the man.

They sat together, yet not together, looking out onto the ocean. The mist had lifted just enough so that he could finally see the lighthouse behind him a short distance from the cliff's edge. On a night like this its beam reflected off the mist, coating the water's surface with a yellowish-white film. Only a few landmarks remained visible, unnaturally illuminated by the beam, and the fog, and the wet. Beside the lighthouse was a two-storey home with many windows on both floors. In the dark and at this distance it might be any home from Ned's village.

"Have you seen my Rhy...? Have you seen an ornament, looks like a clump of mushrooms, green, glows in the dark?" he asked the old guy.

"Nope," the man replied, still staring ahead, "no one and nothin' out here."

The way the man was fixed on the lighthouse beam caused Ned to follow his gaze. When he stood up, Ned stood up. When he moved a step or two closer to the edge, so did a curious Ned. Perhaps it was the echoing of the man's behaviours which made him finally notice. Perhaps the Rhyll had brought him here to notice. In any case Ned did see it. He saw a young woman standing in a flimsy pink dress on the cliff opposite, across the narrow straight. The light shone full on her. She was there, but she wasn't really there. That is to say, he could see her, and he could see through her.

"Is that ... a-a-a ghost?" Ned asked, barely daring to give it a name.

"You see it too lad?" The old man was paying attention to him now. "You can see her?"

"Sure, although I can also see through her," he observed. "What, or who, I am seeing?"

"That's me Gran'," said the man. "She comes here most nights," he added, "Usually it's just me what can see her."

"She's beautiful," Ned observed, "Is she crying do you think?"

"She was very beautiful and she is crying I fear. She cries all the time. She's been crying for sixty years or more since she passed on. In her lifetime she had no time for tears. She had to get on with it, with two babies to raise and a lighthouse to keep all on her own for most of her life. ... She were Finn's wife you see."

"The guy in the song?"

"Yup." Then the man turned away from the cliff and asked, "Would you like to hear their story, the longer version of that song?"

"Oh yes please," said Ned, continuing to stare at the ghostly figure. "What was her name?"

"She were Emily Finnbar, Emily Clark as was. My name's Samuel Finnbar by the way. You can call me Sam."

"Pleased to meet you Sam," Ned replied. "I'm Ned, this is my dog Rufus. Finnbar? You said your grandpa's name was Finn?"

"Well spotted Ned. His name were William Finnbar but everyone called him Finn. Anyway, the reason Emily comes here is that she is still looking for her Finn."

"She lost him?" Ned asked feeling a bit confused.

"More like the sea lost him, or never returned him ...."

"Let me start as it all did many years ago, before I were ever thought of. It would be as much as a hundred years I suppose. Emily and Finn lived in this lighthouse back then. There were no house there at that time. It were Finn's job to keep the light going. Back in them days it were a gaslight, you see.

"As a young lad Finn had been a sailor, just a regular seaman mind, nothing fancy, the kind what does the grunt work. For him that grunt work was on the sailing ship, *The Edwin Casey*. He was pretty light on his feet, so it were up to him to climb the masts when the sails got stuck in the riggin'."

Sam paused for a moment, wincing with pain. "Me bones ache these days." He sat down on the rocks before he continued. "Finn would never talk about the accident much, but from what Emily had been told, and she told me Dad ... It were an awful stormy night; the waters were rough. Finn had been sent up the mast by his Captain, lucky for him as it turned out. Anyway the ship, the captain were likely filled with drink as he usually was, the ship ran right up against these rocks here and it pierced a huge hole in the hull. Finn on the masthead was thrown clear as the ship listed and sank right off. It were so quick that many of his mates below deck were sucked under, stood no chance of escape."

"Just here." Sam rose to his feet and walked to the edge pointing a finger downwards to the straight below. He sighed, "Lives were lost that night, Ned. Finn were washed onto a rock, didn't realize what had happened to his mates until he woke up a couple of days later with concussion, and a broken leg that gave him quite a limp."

"The rest of the crew returned home leaving Finn to recover in the town, that town over there a ways. Even after he was able to walk he stayed on. He still loved the sea, mind you, but he had lost his taste for the work with his bad leg and all ... nor had he ever stopped grieving over the loss of his pals.

"The townsfolk had decided to build a lighthouse to prevent a tragedy of that sort from happening again. They asked Finn to stay on to man it, to be the lighthouse keeper. Finn were grateful for the job. He were committed to preventing the sea and the rocks from taking more lives. He stayed on here for years in this lighthouse."

"He had been living here for about ten years before he saw the girl, Emily as it turned out to be. She would come down to the point just opposite to stand in the glow of the lighthouse beam. Finn would watch out for her, wait for her to show. Well ... he fell in love didn't he, before they'd even met. He looked for her in town. Months it took before he figured a way to introduce himself. Finally he did, many times in fact. And finally she took him up on one of his offers. He courted her for two years or more before she agreed to wed him."

Sam shifted to better view the ghost of Emily as he said, "When I were just a young boy, Ned, Grandma Emily would tell me about how cramped they had been in that lighthouse. They never minded, she said. They were that close to each other, the love were thick between 'em. They had a son in their first year, my Dad it were, and they were expecting another..."

Sam paused, a bit longer this time, until Ned wondered if this was where the story ended. "So ... that night ... when it happened, Finn was minding the lighthouse as per usual. It were a night just as foggy as this one. He were up the tower adjusting the flame when he first heard the cries. He ran to the cliff-face right off. He could make out five folks in a very small dingy trying to land against the sheer rock. They couldn't see the ladder he'd made for the climbing, not in that fog. "He rushed down the ladder onto the dock he'd made years before; called out to them to get them in. And they done it; no trouble getting them to shore. Finn thought it had been a job well done. They were grateful to him of course, falling all over his neck and all. But they were worried sick as well. They told Finn that they'd come off a steamer five kilometres out, well into the ocean. That steamer had been full of timber when a huge swell had shifted its load causing it to lean over like. It were obvious it would sink as it were taking on water even before they set off. In their haste to rescue themselves though one of the two lifeboats had been sunk. There had never been enough lifeboats on the ship to begin with, not for the number of souls aboard. Now ... well the only lifeboat they had was so small that only five could safely get in, even when they were squeezed. They had completely lost their bearings, had no idea where to head for shore. They set off not knowing if they would be lost, leaving thirteen behind on board still, promising to send help if they could.

"Well, Finn couldn't let that happen could he? Especially not after what he'd been through. He asked one of the men from the lifeboat to fetch help from town which were a fair distance away, no cars or motor-craft back then, too long to sensibly wait. He took his own rowboat to which he attached the dingy from the steamer, set off in the direction they'd pointed using only a compass to guide him. It worked! What were the chances? It took him four hours to find the steamer leaning over, riding very low on the waves as it did. He got five into his own boat with five others following him in that life boat.

"But that were only ten he had saved. Three more remained aboard on a steamer that could never have stayed afloat until the morning; it had taken on a lot of water already. The townspeople were waiting by the dock as he came in. He asked them to return with him to save those last three souls. They said it were hopeless, a foolish rescue in such a dark fog, at such a distance, for a steamer with no clear direction to set themselves towards. But Finn turned right back all the same when he dropped the passengers off. He went back to sea in the same direction as before. As he left the dock they shouted after him, 'You're a fool Finn ... but you're a brave one.'"

Sam came to a full stop now, pacing about. "Emily waited all night, all the next day ... and the next ... and the next. He never returned to her ... There she stands most nights now, waiting for him ..."

The solemnity of the moment was seared by Rufus barking. He wasn't just barking as he did to exercise his lungs. This was barking with a purpose. Ned crossed over to him, squinting into the fog. He could see nothing, but he heard two sounds – a loud crack and a splash. "Did you hear that Sam?"

"Nope," Sam replied. "That's you being fanciful 'cuz you just heard my story."

Rufus kept up his barking, bouncing around near the cliff edge. In fact it looked like the dog just might jump over. "Sit! Stay! Quiet!" Ned commanded as he listened even more intently. It wasn't much but there was a noise that could have been splashing. It was hard to tell over the natural lapping of water on rocks. "Sam, I think there may something out there. But I need to get closer to tell. Rufus is making too much of a fuss for it to be nothing."

"I tell you it is nothing Ned. Sounds come from there all the time."

"Do you want to be like the townsfolk Sam, or do you want to be like Finn?"

"When you put like that ... There's a ladder what goes down the cliff just there. At the bottom there's a dock with a rowboat tied to it."

Ned took a deep breath before he stepped onto the ladder. He'd been up and down a couple of ladders before; still he got 'the willies' each time. "How far down Sam?" he asked as he stepped onto the first rung.

"At a guess – ten metres?"

"He's guessing – he's not sure?" Ned thought grimly. It was when he was about five metres down he figured that he heard the plaintive voice.

"Now even I heard that!" shouted Sam. "I'm coming down too."

Ned reached the bottom, quickly stripping down to his loca-hamour suit. Then he looked back up the ladder at the ancient fellow with the sore bones, trying to climb down a sheer cliff on a swinging rope ladder that had been a tough go even for a fit boy. When Sam reached the dock Ned rushed forward saying, "I'm so sorry I dared you like that."

"Nonsense boy you couldn't have stopped me." Then in full rescue mode Sam took charge. "Right lad, let me get in the boat first to steady her by the dock. Then you untie her and get your-self in. I'll hold her steady don't you worry." Now that they were right on the water they could hear the cries very distinctly. "Keep shouting," Sam called back to the voice in the fog. "We can't see you, but we can row to where your voice is."

They were almost on top of the young woman before they had even seen her. She was floundering, looking quite spent. Between the two of them, though, they got her into the boat. "My husband," she gulped, "Please find him too? I think I saw him over near the rocks on the other side."

"Look Sam," said Ned, now that he had his sea-legs, "It's no distance. I can see the other side from here. I think I see the man as well. Why don't you wait here, leave me to swim over to him."

"No Ned! I could never do that."

"Please Sam, I'm an excellent swimmer. I can hold my breath like no one on earth." Ned slipped into the cold sea water, Indigo under tongue. "Make lots of noise so I know where you are. Sing that song you sang before." He streaked his way easily across to the rocks opposite. It may have been cold, the night air thick, but the water's surface was calm. He easily found the man clinging to the rocks quite spent from his ordeal. "He's here Sam, I've found him! Come in a bit closer with the boat now, not as far as these rocks though. They're quite sharp here. No wonder *The Edwin Casey* went down."

"I'm okay," said the swimmer, in a panting tone. "I just need to get my bearings for a second ... and my breath. If that man keeps singing we could swim to the boat now don't you think?"

Within minutes Sam had found them and had pulled them both aboard. "Now, I just need to find that dock ..." he said.

"Really?"

"Nope," Sam replied with a wink, "I can get us back with me eyes shut."

The shipwrecked couple were out of breath, in shock and a bit banged up. With a few minutes to recover on the dock, however, they found just enough strength to climb the ladder to safe ground. Ned couldn't help noticing how slowly Sam climbed back up that ladder though. The exertion had taken its toll on the elder. It was obvious his muscles and joints were straining. He waited below until he saw Sam safely back before he started up himself.

Topside, he lay back resting on his elbows in a glow of self-satisfaction. It had all gone smoothly; he was proud of himself. *Now to find the Rhyll*, he mused. *It must be close at hand ...* When Rufus started up with the barking again he felt dismay. Reluctantly he pulled himself to his feet and caught up with the drenched couple who Sam was leading back to his home. "Were you two the only ones in the boat?"

"Yes ... no... We had our dog with us ... Ned!"

"How do you know my name is Ned?" he asked.

"No, no .... The dog's name ... *Ned*."

"That settles it," he said, whipping his clothes off once more. "Has it got red hair as well?"

"What? No ... White with brown patches ... a Jack Russell."

"I'm rescuing it just the same. Sam, will you sing out again? I won't go out any farther than your voice can reach. That way I will be able to find my way back." He started back down the ladder, despite Sam's shouts of, "You're a fool young Ned ... but you're a brave one."

He hadn't thought the complete plan through. By the time he reached the bottom, however, he had a couple more pieces in place, as he called up, "You see that knapsack near Rufus, Sam?"

"Yup," Sam shouted down.

"Empty it will you, toss it down?"

"You say so lad."

Ned put the knapsack over his shoulders before getting into the boat. He didn't know how far from shore he would have to go to find the dog; he didn't know how to retrieve it when or if he did. He rowed clumsily, inexpertly into the gap calling out as he went. He called for the dog; it was Sam who answered each time. Ned flapped about not knowing where he was, or even where he had been before he heard the faint whimper. Then he saw on top of a capsized small motorboat the little dog scared, not daring to move.

How to get the dog into the boat though? It was terrified, wouldn't budge. Ned jumped from his boat and swam to the dog who sat shivering, balancing to keep itself upright. Calling out in a calm voice to little Ned he tried to coax the dog to jump to him. He could see that the frightened dog wouldn't, or couldn't, leave his perch. He pulled himself back into the rowboat tying the painter of the capsized craft to his own like Finn had done in Sam's story. He rowed as straight as he could in the direction of Sam's song, his shoulders aching from the strain. When he reached the dock, Ned tied up the rowboat slipping into the water again. He circled around the motorboat pushing and pulling away at it until one side just touched the dock. He pulled himself out, yanking the damaged boat even closer until the little dog finally took courage, leaped and landed with a bit of a flop on the dock.

Ned scooped up the dog, holding it close to let his lochamour suit warm it. "Here little Ned, this is what I do to calm Rufus. I stroke his neck just like this, see?" He knew the dog had to be much calmer, braver, before he tried his next trick. He called up to the others that he and the dog were both fine, to just give them a few minutes more.

"Now I'm just going to put you in this sack," he explained, like the dog could understand him. It was a bit a struggle, but he managed to do it and he tied the flap down just in case. The sack was almost more than he could hoist over his shoulders with a little dog inside, let alone carry any distance. He couldn't ask the man or woman to do it; they were in rough shape themselves. Sam was spent from his heroic efforts earlier on. So Ned did it! He hunched the bag onto his back and climbed that ten metre ladder under his own steam with a squirmy dog tied to his back! When he got halfway to the top, for some reason he could never explain, he turned to look back and saw – a green glow deep within the water.

***

"Sam," Ned said softly, when the couple and their dog had finally left the house and gone back to town by taxi. They were seated now at the quaint kitchen table in Sam's home. "Sam," he repeated," I need to go back down to the dock I'm afraid. I've left something behind."

"Are you mad?" Sam exclaimed, "Wait 'til morning can't you?"

"That's just it, I can't wait," he replied, "and I can't tell you why."

Sam closed his eyes, slumped down in his chair, and sighed a deep sigh. "Okay lad. I'll come with ya."

"I hate to ask it Sam," he said, "but it would help if you could stand on the cliff and sing out, just in case I lose my way."

"Cup of tea first?" Sam asked, pulling the pot from the shelf.

"Absolutely," Ned replied, taking the small sack from around his neck to retrieve – another half unicorn hair.

Ned took his third swim of the evening, this time to the bottom of the straight just beyond the dock. He found the Rhyll easily of course, just as it had intended. He found something else besides. He found Finn, or the ghost of him, keeping guard over the wreck of *The Edwin Casey,* the ship that held the souls of his mates.

Ned didn't need the Rhyll to tell him what he had to do then. He swam right up to Finn, looked him full in his transparent face, mouthing *Em-il-y.* Then he grabbed for the Rhyll with one arm motioning to Finn to follow him to the surface. Maybe it was because he was holding a Rhyll, or maybe Finn understood when he mouthed her name, or maybe he was just finally ready to move. But the ghost of Finn did follow Ned, and by doing so, looked up for the first time in more than a century.

***

"Sam," Ned said softly, as they sat together on the cliff.

"Yes lad," Sam replied wearily.

"I don't know where Finn went down at sea but I do know where he's been all this time. And I know where he is now," he said, nodding his head towards the cliff opposite. Finn's ghost walked into the lighthouse beam to stand behind his wife. She turned to see ... ran to him ... they misted away.

Chapter Eight:
Neville in the North

At the full moon in September, six months after he had met Sam, Ned began working on another theory. He was sure that it was only at full moons when he would meet with the Rhyll but now he thought that there might be more rules that he hadn't figured on.

He didn't see the Rhyll every full moon. So what else would determine when they were off on adventures? Maybe only when it was a clear night? No because there were clear nights with full moons when he hadn't seen the Rhyll. What's more this past March had been quite foggy and cold when the Rhyll had appeared.

He sketched it out on a piece of paper, months on one side, adventures in the middle, and on the other, his age at the time of the adventures. He could think of no more details than these...

January .... *nothing*
February....... *nothing*
March .... *saved 2 people and dog from drowning,*
with Sam .... *12 yrs. old*
April.............. *nothing*
May .... *rescued Aqua-Marie from being*
sold at market .... *10 yrs. old*
June .... *helped some sick elves; helped*
return a stink home .... *11 yrs. old*

July.............. got unicorn to donate tail hairs
for horse medicine .... 11 yrs. old
August.......... nothing
September.... nothing
October .... vision quest with Rhyll;
learned a bit of its language........ 12 yrs. old
November..... faced down bully Branwen with
Elam, Kiri & Butterwort................ 11 yrs. old
December..... nothing

He had been on six adventures in three years if you counted the time he spent on the vision-quest in his own garden, which he did. Was there any more of a pattern to be seen here? What about the number of adventures per year?

First year – 3
Second year – 2
Third year – 1, so far

So the number per year didn't seem to be a factor. What about the number by age?

Age 10 – 1
Age 11 – 3
Age 12 – 2

He was thirteen now so that wasn't it either. What about adventures by months of the year? Ned studied this one carefully. He had been on six adventures in six different months: March, May, June, July, October, November. That could mean he got one adventure for each month of the year – twelve adventures. If this was right he still had six adventures to go in the months of January, February, April, August, September and December. *I'm definitely going to be checking this theory out with the Rhyll.*

***

If he had to choose just one favourite friend from his Rhyll adventures, Ned reflected much later in life, it would have been Neville. He loved all of them to be sure. He missed them all as well. But Neville ... Neville was unique! Not that he took to him right off, not in those first few moments. In fact, being influenced by all those stories he'd read, Ned feared for his life at first. As soon as he realized how special Neville was, what a one-of-a-kinder, what a truly big heart, he wanted to become best friends with the guy who was a bit of a loner as Ned had once been.

It was January and he was thirteen when he met Neville, ten months since his last trip with the Rhyll. In weak moments Ned did wonder if the Rhyll had finished with him, though mostly he knew that it would come back. He had this theory after all, that he had six more adventures to go. So he relaxed for the most part and enjoyed his life, his family, his friends, keeping one eye open at full moons.

He always credited his best friend Maeve for the fact that he had more than one friend now. There were the kids from around Island Lake, Maeve's friends first, now his friends too. Although they were still better ice skaters than he was, he was the better swimmer, even without the Indigo. With the confidence he felt in this group, other friendships became easier – from school, especially from Science Club. In Science Club Ned got to meet fellow astronomers who liked watching the night sky as he did. The telescope he had gotten for his birthday two years before needed a stronger lens now if he were to search farther out into space, maybe as far away as where Rhylls once lived. There was this one boy in the Club who had a great telescope who would invite Ned over to use it. So all in all, his thirteenth year had been pretty good and it wasn't over yet!

He had been eying the pot with the crackle glaze and the snowflake design for some months now. "I'd quite like to go somewhere with snow next time, improve my skating. Maybe if I asked the Rhyll, and didn't just throw it into a pot with a particular design on it?"

After each adventure he re-stocked his tins and jars, using his allowance money so his Mom wouldn't wonder. He prepared for colder weather just in case, putting even warmer clothes in the trunk. Besides the blanket Kiri had given him, Ned stored his sleeping bag there now.

Yet in spite of all his anticipation and his theory, Ned was amazed to see the Rhyll peeking up through snow, this time in the January full moon. He had to scratch his head really hard to keep it in mind, as he imagined it pushing up through frozen earth, that the Rhyll wasn't actually a plant. He knew it was true, still to see it there in his frozen garden was mystifying. Being prepared, he acted quickly, grabbed his skates, put on his warmest coat, toque, mittens, scarf, and boots, and left on the run.

He had already decided to leave Rufus behind this time. Rufus was 10 years old now; in dog years that was creaky. He felt sure he would be skating because he would ask the Rhyll directly to take him to a skating pond. If he were to be in the cold for a long time – well, old Rufus would not enjoy that. Besides, Ned was more used to adventures now – maybe even a bit braver.

He not feel at all brave when he stepped out of the greenhouse right in front of a polar bear and a yeti. *Yipe*! were his first and second thoughts about where he found himself this time. He seriously considered the wisdom of turning right back and shutting himself in the greenhouse. In fact he did just that, barred the door with a few bags of Dad's soil, heart thumping up into his brain and pumping down into his boots.

"Hello?" said a voice. "Have you come for a visit ... or a short stay perhaps? You needn't worry. The bear's asleep, won't wake up 'til March I shouldn't think."

Now who would be out there with that yeti and bear? Ned wondered. It was a well-spoken voice, cultured like his Dad's who had been university-trained.

The voice came again. "Are you still there? My name's Neville ... I welcome you whoever you are. In fact I'd rather enjoy a bit of company. Do you play chess at all?"

"No," Ned's really small voice.

"No matter," said the voice, "I can teach you how. Would you like a game of chess?"

"Um ... what about that yeti? Is it friendly?"

"I am 'that yeti' as you call me. I am very friendly. I'm vegetarian; is that friendly enough for you?"

Ned considered. The Rhyll wouldn't bring him to a place that meant certain death. Also he needed to find his 'ticket' home. "Okay ... I-I-I'm coming out now."

As he opened the greenhouse door, Ned was looking directly into the face of the yeti, who had stooped over in a bow, head forward, smiling. He had the kindest face, quite handsome too in a very hairy way. He was giant-sized, well-built with bulging muscles everywhere – legs, arms, chest, neck. His fur which covered most of his body was a sable brown, clean and well-brushed. His deep brown eyes were so soft and kind that they seemed to be melting, even in all this cold.

"Helloooooo," the yeti said. "I'm Neville. The polar bear is Frigitte. She's hibernating before she becomes a mother again. She won't bother us. I just like to give her a place to sleep it off each year."

"I'm Ned Clery. I'm human."

"Hello Ned," Neville replied, in the friendliest of tones. "It's been a while since I entertained. I'm human too, or humanoid I guess you would say ... I've got a bit of frozen vegetable stew on a stick if you'd like."

"That might be nice Neville ... a bit later perhaps." Ned couldn't imagine stew on a stick; then there were lots of things he'd eaten that he hadn't imagined would be good, so he kept an open mind.

"Have you come for that green glowing thing over there by Frigitte?" Neville asked. "It arrived a few minutes ago about the same time as you, so I wondered if it belonged to you. It looks a bit like magic. Is it magic Ned?"

Well if the Rhyll had plunked itself down almost next to Neville, he reasoned, then he needed an explanation. The truth, however bizarre, was always best. "It is, Neville, it is magic."

"Right then," said Neville, "we'll just leave it by Frigitte for now shall we? It seems pretty happy there. Why don't you have a seat?" he said pointing to an ice chair. "Pull the animal skins around you so you don't freeze."

Ned took a moment to look about while he sat there trying to get warm. He was in a cave, the walls, ceiling and floor of which were entirely made of ice and snow. He was sitting on an ice chair, in fact all of the furniture was made of ice, chiselled in a tasteful modern design. Animal skins covered the seats and backs of some of the chairs; there were piles of furs on a bed made of ice as well. Mid-cavern, hanging down from the ceiling amongst the many icicles, was a chandelier made of twigs on which had been attached candle holders. Candle power seemed to be the single light source for the place. On a coffee table made of ice as well, in a very stylish sitting area, was a chess set which showed a game-in-progress. Cluttered about on the table and floor were stacks of books. Except for the messiness of the books, this frozen cavern could have been showcased in any home decorating magazine.

Ned was still sizing the yeti up, when Neville spoke again, "Seeing you there in those animal skins reminds me of my father. He could never be too warm. He loved it here, mind you, but he never got used to the cold."

"I thought yetis liked the cold."

"Oh Dad wasn't a yeti. He was as ordinarily human as you. He was an airplane pilot when he met my mother. She was a yeti, though she preferred to be called North-Polian. So that makes me a yeti-human hybrid I guess, but I prefer North-Polian too.

"Dad was in the Air Force. It was his job to drop supplies off to the research and weather station in Nunavut from time to time. On one of these missions, the last as it turned out to be, in the dark winter months, he got caught in sudden bad weather which blew him off-course. He must have been a great pilot because he did a "controlled crash" as they call it. He survived, just barely. He had been knocked so far off-course that he ended up here at the pole. I imagine they tried to find him but they wouldn't have looked this far out. Besides in those rough weather conditions, they'd have given up the search pretty quickly.

"Mom found him almost dead, covered in snow, and brought him back here. He was unconscious for ten days after the crash. When he did awaken he was still very ill – broken bones, frost bite and blind, temporarily thank goodness. Mom stayed by his side the whole time, wouldn't let him out of her sight. He fell in love with her gentle spirit when he was blind; he remained in love with her generous heart even after his sight was restored.

"It was Dad who gave me the love of books. He home-schooled me starting with just the one book he brought with him on the plane, Robinson Crusoe. That's pretty funny don't you think? A story about a guy shipwrecked, befriending a native, same as Dad. Anyway he taught me to read with that book."

"You have so many books. Where did you get them all?"

"I got them from Santa."

"What! *The* Santa?"

Neville chuckled, "Ah, you think you're too old to believe in Santa do you? Too bad 'cuz I was going to introduce you to him."

"Wow!" Ned burst out, "I'm going have to re-think Christmas again."

"I have asked Santa for books every year since I learned to read," Neville explained, "starting with a set of encyclopedias. Ten years it took to get the complete set. That's how I have learned about the world, a world I have never seen. After that I asked for some of the classics so that I could see what good writing was all about."

He sat down on the sofa next to Ned's chair, his fingers stroking his books on the coffee table before he went on. "Santa gave me this chess set too as his special gift to me. It was he who taught me to play. I'll teach you if you like. Or ... we could take a tour of North Pole Pax Inc.

"Where Santa lives?"

"It's much more than that Ned. I'll let him explain shall I? Would you enjoy that do you think? There's a tunnel from my place that connects to the main building."

"Would I? What kid wouldn't?"

***

North Pole Pax Inc.... Whatever Ned ever imagined it was, he thought much differently after this. They entered the first workshop through a carved wooden door leading up from Neville's tunnel. You could have put Ned's entire village inside this one building, it was that big. Assembly-lines made with brass fittings and painted wooden parts were crowded with toys in the making. Each time a toy entered one of the wondrous machines, it came out the other side with another intriguing piece added. At the end of each line were huge finishing tables, carved and painted with flying reindeer, big clumps of holly with luscious red berries, brass bells strung with ribbon – in fact everything Ned had always thought of as Christmas. Seated around each finishing table, elves were adding tiny details to toys, checking to see that they worked, packaging them for shipping.

"How big of an operation is this Neville?" Ned asked when he recovered his use of speech.

"There must be a hundred of these types of buildings," Neville explained, "Then there are the stables, warehouses, elf apartments, homes. Santa's own place is quite small by comparison. It's city-sized here at North Pole Pax Inc."

Ned expected Santa's elves to be tiny with pointy hats and shoes like the stories he'd read, the pictures he'd seen. In actual fact they came in all sizes. They resembled the sylvans and root-elves, in that their skin was waxy and all the men were bald. Unlike the sylvans, their skin colour did not match their outfits though. Since they didn't need to camouflage themselves as the forest elves did for protection their clothing could be more colourful. It seemed at the North Pole, the more colourful, the better. Red and green were quite popular colours as Ned expected, although all colours of the rainbow were represented. They had no uniforms, preferring to dress as they pleased and as suited their individual tastes.

"Can I introduce you to a particular friend Ned?" Neville asked, as they came to the centre of the shop. "This is Crispin my father's best friend, now mine as well."

Crispin was an elderly elf of unimaginable years. He was very craggy like the root-elves, but with a ruddy red face. He was quite tall although Neville was at least two heads taller than he, and he was pleasantly plump. He was dressed in a deep purple suit made of velvet with a lime green shirt underneath. A striped woollen scarf of red, blue and green was wrapped around his throat twice and he wore a bright green toque over his wrinkled bald head. On his feet he wore heavy leather black boots with yellow laces.

"Ned is it?" Crispin said. "So glad you've come. Where have you come from by the way?"

"From a small village about the size of this building," Ned explained. "I'm sure it would be south of here."

"Crispin and Dad were great business partners, Ned," Neville explained. "What those two did to improve the North Pole can't go unspoken!"

"You embarrass me youngster," Crispin blushed.

"Crispin and Dad developed the thermal shield that protects us from the harshest of the winter weather. It drops the temperature by about 40 degrees, from -43° Celsius to a balmy -3° on an average day. It cuts down on the wind chill as well. It helps heat the buildings and lights the assembly lines in winter. We can do more things now – make more toys, play outside ...”

"Your Dad was a wonderful man to be sure. I miss him every day. But you are quite as wonderful," Crispin said proudly. "Neville helps me run the gears in the place. He supplies us all with vegetables too. Has he shown you his greenhouse?”

"You have a greenhouse?”

"My proudest achievement Ned! Would like to see?”

"I've got a greenhouse ... and a little garden of my own," Ned explained. "Not in the winter of course.”

"Well mine's not very big in the winter. Still I can grow some crops under the special lights Dad and Crispin invented.”

Neville's greenhouse was bigger than Ned's parents' entire property, plus the next door neighbour's, plus the one after that. Most of it was empty flats on carts at the moment, over the dark winter months. One area about the size of Ned's living room at home was planted with vegetables under grow lights. The greenhouse was made of glass, triple-paned to keep out the cold. Each type of vegetable had its own thick wooden flat elevated about a metre off the ground. Giant water barrels with spigots hung from the ceiling on heavy iron bars above the flats. Hoses had been attached to each spigot for watering the vegetables. Extra garden supplies were neatly stacked in one corner next to a planting table, much like Ned's father's, only bigger. The temperature of the air was chilly though not freezing.

"Right," Neville said, rubbing his palms together. "I've got winter-hardy vegetables growing now Ned." His eyes were highly animated, his voice proud. "Broccoli, leeks, cabbages, kale. In summer, when it is daylight all the time, I can grow tomatoes, carrots, cucumbers, onions, lettuces. I have an herb garden as well. It gets quite warm in here in summer with the sun beating in all the time. I have tried to be a bit adventurous over the years with more exotic vegetables, but I have now decided to stick to the ones that everyone likes. I've never grown much fruit, however. I long to grow fruit – beyond a few berries that is. It doesn't really work to grow anything bigger, because trees and bushes don't do well in the greenhouse. I can't plant them deep enough you see. The planters are too shallow."

"I plant my seeds outdoors Neville. Dad keeps a few tomato plants in our greenhouse though."

"It's never warm enough at the Pole to plant outdoors. There is no natural soil here either, only ice and snow. Every speck of soil and mulch has been brought in by Santa. I just give him a list to add to the groceries he picks up after his Christmas deliveries. Speaking of which would you like to meet him now?"

***

Santa Claus was just as Ned pictured him from all the Christmas stories. He was larger than life in every way. Seated in a high-backed leather chair in front of a fireplace, in a study full of books, he chewed on an unlit corn cob pipe. His hair was long, curly and snowy white, as was his beard which hung over a fair sized belly. His trousers were red velvet and his shirt was white with tiny holly berries on each button. Although he didn't have on his usual coat, hat or boots, this was the very image of the jolly man that Ned knew.

"Ah yes Ned. I was told you were coming by for a visit. From the way you are looking at me I am just what you expected. Am I right?"

"Yes sir."

"Of course," Santa said with a wink, "I am what you expected. What about now?" he asked, turning one complete circle. His appearance had changed to that of a tall thin man in a white beard and a hooded red velvet long coat. "I am Father Christmas now from Great Britain." Turning again he still looked a bit like Father

Christmas, but his robes had turned a rich blue. "I am Ded Moroz, as they call me in Russia." At the next turnabout his beard had become a bit trimmer and he was in a white robe, a red cape and a tall red hat. "I am St. Nicholas, the Dutch Santa." As he kept spinning around each time he looked different; each time he introduced himself by a different name, from a different country.

"Wow!" Ned exclaimed. "You are all those people?"

"There are more Ned. I re-suit myself to appeal to many cultures. Furthermore North Pole Pax Inc. is only one of a chain of world-wide organizations that make toys."

Santa sat down again in his comfy chair motioning to Ned and Neville to sit in the two chairs to either side. Then he filled mugs with steaming hot chocolate that had been left in a large coffee-pot on a low table in front of the chairs.

"Now where were we? Ah yes I was going to ask you a question. What do you think Santa, in all my names and forms, is all about?"

"Is he about surprising children, making them happy by giving them their favourite toys?"

"That's certainly very fun isn't it? Would it surprise you to know that it isn't really about toys at all?"

"I think that would surprise me Santa, yes. Then is it about a magical man who comes to us one day each year to make us all feel very special?"

"Perhaps there is a bit of that in it too Ned. I think of myself as just an ordinary man though who has the use of extraordinary magical tools."

"Then why do you spend your whole life making toys to give away?"

"Imagine a world that gets a bit lost, where people sometimes worry about each other because we don't all look the same or have the same traditions, a world where people sometimes even go to war over these differences."

"I don't like to think about that very much. I don't understand war at all."

"Nor do I Ned ... and I am hundreds of years old! Imagine though one moment each year when these worries stop; a moment when people pay more attention to loving their children than to fearing each other; a moment when men of war lay down their guns for a brief time, as they remember that they were children once too."

"Is that what North Pole Pax Inc. is about?" Ned asked. He was beginning to understand what Santa was saying.

"Precisely," said Santa. "I am so proud of you Ned. Children are the key to North Pole Pax Inc. We all love our children, want them to be happy. For one day each year we celebrate this. And, for maybe just one second in that one day each year, the whole world imagines peace at the very same time ... Just imagine."

Ned sat silently for a few minutes sipping his hot chocolate before he answered, "I will imagine that Santa – at least one day a year."

"That is all I ask."

***

"Boy that Santa sure is a nice guy," Ned exclaimed as he completed his seventh twirl on the perfectly smooth ice. They had come outdoors to a not unbearably cold landscape with a frozen lake that seemed to go on forever. Although Neville had no skates of his own, he was pleased to slide about the ice while Ned and the others skated. The others were workshop elves on a break, and ice-fairies dressed in cool blues with colourful gossamer wings and tiny skates.

Not surprisingly the fairies were the best skaters. With wings on their backs they were unlikely to fall which made them more daring, lighter on their feet. Their twirls defined grace and defied gravity, as they inevitably ended up twirling so hard that they became airborne. They loved Ned as all fairies seemed to. They tried to give him a few lessons and found him a very willing pupil.

In fact he was so sad when Neville called him to come in saying, "Sometimes you humans forget just how cold it is on ice and, before you know it, you're nursing frost-bite on your little parts – toes, fingers and noses." So they returned to Neville's home where the yeti almost smothered him in furs and went off to the main building to fetch more hot chocolate.

Ned was just coming to grips with the rules of chess, when an alarm bell jarred them both from their chairs. "That's the emergency alarm Ned. I must go."

"Can I come too?"

"Yes ... try to keep up though."

***

"I don't understand it Neville ... Santa." Crispin was explaining to each man, in a very strained voice. "We had enough solar opals to last the season, but when I went in to replace some of the tired ones there were no fresh ones left. Absolutely none!"

"You have found no explanation?" Neville asked, looking very concerned, "No clues lying about?"

"None that I can see," Crispin replied, his shoulders very stooped with stress, "How can we do without the opals until summer?"

"We have done without before," Santa soothed the elf, "although it will slow down production a great deal as we will have to close down a number of our workshops to conserve energy. The greenhouse will lose its power as well I'm afraid Neville. And of course the harsher weather outside will keep us all indoors for months. We will have to lower the heat and lighting to the buildings, and wear more layers of clothing. Also we will have to insist that the ice-fairies come inside from the cold. We will need to make space for them. They only moved to the Pole, Ned," Santa explained, "after we got the thermal shield; they will never survive in the much colder and windier weather."

"Shouldn't you try to find the 'solar opals', is that what you called them, first?" Ned asked.

"Quite right," Neville agreed. "If there are no visible clues maybe I can pick up a scent or two." With this Neville got down on all fours, placed his nose close to the bin, sniffed it and the floor all about in a very wide circle. "Hmmm," he concluded. "Barely a scent."

"Aha!" cried Crispin and Santa together. "That's clear then isn't it?" Crispin said, to which Santa sadly nodded.

"It's not clear to me," Ned added, scratching his toque, "What does it mean?"

"It means fairies, I'm afraid Ned, or perhaps just one," Neville explained, shaking his head. "They are so tiny and because they fly, they leave almost no scent or trail on the ground."

"How will you find out which of them stole the opals? How will you get the opals back?"

"We love having our fairies around," said Crispin, "but we don't know very much about them. They like staying outside, making their homes in our rafters you see. We feed them of course; let them take whatever else they need. In fact they are allowed in all the workshops. They work for Jack Frost though, so they remain outside ice painting our doors and windows."

"I know a couple of fairies," Ned remarked.

"You do?" Santa said, clearly impressed. "What an amazing boy you are!"

"Oh no," Ned replied," I'm just an ordinary boy.... who has had the use of extraordinary magical tools. Isn't that right Santa?"

"Ho-ho, clever boy! What do you know about fairies then?"

"I know fairies are cheeky. When they get flustered they can be positively rude. The ones I knew had good hearts, however, meant no harm. They didn't always want to do the right thing at first, but they were easily persuaded if you reasoned with them. Oh, I know one more thing about fairies ... They like cake."

***

"Just what are solar opals, Neville," Ned asked as they were laying out the last of the dishes on the big party table. Mrs. Claus and some of the baker elves had prepared a sweet feast. There were the usual cookies, candies, and sugar plums, but loads of iced cakes as well. Warm punches and hot chocolate would be laid out just as the guests arrived.

"Solar opals? They are crystals that hold the energy of the sun. Santa was given a big sack of them years ago as a gift by a grateful King Magupu, when he was making his deliveries in the tropics one year. So we don't know precisely where they came from, only the general area. Santa was just using them to decorate the place before my Dad discovered their energy potential. So Dad worked with Crispin who was in charge of the machinery – all the gizmos, gadgets and thingamabobs. The two of them developed technology that made use of the opals' energy to improve our lives here.

"The opals are rechargeable you see. We leave them out during our six months of sunshine and they re-energize by absorbing the summer's ultra-violet rays. Then, when we are plunged into six months of darkness, the crystals energize the whole place, the shield as well, until we see the sun and feel that speck of warmth return. We can survive without them, we have done so before. However, the number of children in the world is ever increasing. It will make things very difficult to get all the toys done for next year without more solar opals. But there's our comforts that we will miss also ... and our vegetables," he added with a sigh.

"Well maybe we can reason with the fairies or at least solve the mystery of the opals' disappearance during this party," Ned observed.

What an absolute smash of a party it was! Ned had never been to a celebration quite this huge before. He was surprised at how comfortable he felt amongst all these folks, given that they were strangers for the most part. But then he had been treated so very well from the first. He couldn't begin to count all the elves, and he loved watching the ice-fairies flying about grabbing sweets from the tables, plunging into the punch bowls.

When the festivities were in full swing Santa clanged a big bell. "Now I don't want to spoil any of the fun of the evening," he announced with his usual twinkle. "I do have some news to share with you all, however, something I'm afraid that will affect us over the next few months. It seems we have lost a number of our solar opals."

"What are solar opals?" asked a fairy voice, giggly from all the sweets.

"Solar opals are small white stones that glow and give off coloured lights, warmth, and a great deal of energy." Santa explained. "We rather need them to run North Pole Pax Inc., I'm afraid. Without them, things will have to change ... for the worse."

"Change how?" Another fairy voice, a little worried.

"You fairies are going to have to move indoors with us first off. It will become unbearably cold outside because the thermal shield will fail soon."

The ice-fairies huddled together in conference after which six of them raced off returning in minutes with six opals – each hugging onto one as they flew. "We had no idea what they were for," confessed one fairy, laying her jewel on Santa's palm.

"We use them for heating and lighting our homes," explained Eirlys, King of the ice-fairies. "We are not plugged into to your main power source at the Pole. We get cold. We had no idea what you used them for. Apologies, Santa."

"Thank you," Santa replied. With all six in his hand he added, "This is only a few though. They will keep us going for a little while longer, but we need to find the rest if we are to keep everything going until spring."

"It wasn't us Santa," said King Eirlys defensively. "This is all we borrowed."

"I believe you of course ... Let us continue with the party for now, solve the mystery later."

Ned walked amongst the party-goers doing what he did best – just watching. In one hand he carried a piece of chocolate chip cake with chocolate icing on a moulded glass plate. He watched, specifically the fairies, especially for fairies not easily seen. It wasn't long before he found what he was looking for – one young fairy lad who was hiding behind some packed boxes in a dark corner far away from the fun.

"Hello," Ned said in his tiniest voice, "I'm Ned ... I have cake. Would you like a bite?"

***

"He didn't know what he was doing," Ned explained to Neville, as they hunched over their chess game sucking vegetable stew on a stick. "He thought the opals were fun. He figured that he'd invented a way to explore outside the dome. He would hold one in his arms as he flew under the thermal shield into the fierce wind and cold, just exploring really. The opal would keep him warm and light his way. After each adventure he would bury the opal in deep snow at the outside edge of the shield. He marked it each time with a twig and a bit of red ribbon. Each time he went out to find it again it would be gone, blown away by the winter gales. So he would get another and another ... until they were all gone. He is so young ... he didn't know better."

"So where are the opals now?" Neville asked.

"All blown away goodness knows where," he replied. "I doubt even magic could find them, not in all the vast space of snow and wind that no living creature could endure, not even yetis."

"Hmmm," said Neville, moving his Knight close to Ned's King on the chessboard. "Check."

***

"I'm going to have to leave soon Neville."

"No Ned, please don't go. I love your company, your stories of the outer world."

"I have to Neville," Ned reasoned, "The Rhyll never lets me stay long. The day will not dawn 'til I go."

"The day won't dawn until late March Ned," Neville observed. "That's hardly an argument at the North Pole."

"I think that time must also stop somehow Neville. So I can't stay ... besides I would miss my own life ... Would you like to see my greenhouse before I go."

"Somewhere new to see?" Neville exclaimed. "Well that's as exciting as Christmas to me."

So Ned steered Neville through the greenhouse door which of course from the outside was invisible to him. Before they went in, Ned scooped up the Rhyll from behind a sleeping Frigitte, carrying it with them inside. "This is my garden," he explained as they looked back out through the glass. "It's covered in snow right now, but you can see some of the evergreens are still growing and the other trees, leaf-less right now, are sleeping. Over there is my garden. At the back is Rufus' doghouse ... he stays inside when it's cold. And way back – that's my house, the top window is my bedroom."

"Amazing!" whistled Neville, "so cute, compact ... and very pretty Ned. I wish to travel beyond the Pole some day.... How will you get home?"

"With the Rhyll. It brings me here in the greenhouse. Then it takes me home again."

"How wonderful! May I see it closer?"

Neville had his fingers on it already, found its vision-chords right away on his own. He was smiling, chattering away and he seemed to be answering questions, as if he had been asked.

"What are you saying? What is it saying?"

"Oh sorry Ned we were speaking yeti. Did you know that it could speak yeti?"

"I didn't know it could speak at all!"

"Oh yes, very well. It wants me to tell you *twelve in all*. Does that mean anything to you?"

"It means I was right! I get twelve adventures in all – one for each month of the year. I knew it!" The Rhyll twinkled and hummed.

"Yes it says you are quite clever. I agree," said Neville. "It says if you want to hear its voice, you need to be quieter."

"What does that mean?" cried Ned, "I'm the quietest kid in my class!"

"I think it means you need to make your brain go quiet," Neville said, as he pulled his fingers away. "I envy you all your adventures in the big wide world Ned. How do you choose where to go?"

"Mostly the Rhyll chooses, but I get a vote. I choose the flowerpot and ..." His voice trailed off in thought. "You know Neville ... I just might have the 'spore' of an idea..."

Chapter Nine:
Neville in the South

Neville shouted down to Ned, who was clinging for dear life at the end of his arm, "Let the bag go Ned! You can't lose your life for a knapsack of trinkets."

"You know it's than more that – much more," Ned said, beads of sweat rolling down his legs and into the molten lava below.

***

Ned was fighting feelings of jealousy. Why had the Rhyll begun speaking to Neville right off, when it hadn't spoken to him yet? Not in words anyway. He sat on the stool at the end of the planting table in a meditative pose making contact with the Rhyll.

"What are we doing Ned?" Neville asked.

"I'm clearing my brain. You need to be quiet!" he said peevishly.

"Sorry," Neville replied, sitting down in a far corner of the greenhouse, "though you'll never hear it with that attitude."

"You're right Neville ... I'm sorry." He started an inward battle with his brain.

Okay now think happy thoughts ... no don't think at all ... let your mind go blank ... don't think about magic, about Maeve, about dogs and parents, about Christmas, about anything ... Oh it's no good. Not wanting to think is harder than it looks. Not wanting to think makes me want to think! I give up!

"Precisely."

Chapter Nine

What? Is that you Rhyll?

"Exactly."

But how? ... Why? ... I mean why now? I'd given up.

"That is what you needed to do Ned ... Greetings."

Hello Rhyll, thank you for all my adventures.

"It has been our pleasure."

Our? There is more than one of you?

"We are a collection of beings – from another world as you know by now. In our language Rhyll means 'community', like your own village in fact. We are a community and we have been pleased to venture with you these past three Earth years. But now you have another challenge for us perhaps?"

Oh yes, although it's so tempting to just keep talking with you. But ... Santa and the guys here at the Pole are in trouble. Their solar opal supply has run down and I wondered if we could find more for them. It's kind of important, maybe even critical. 'Magic seeks magic', I already know that. Are solar opals magic Rhyll?

"There is a magical quality about them, yes Ned. But they are also one of the natural wonders of Earth. We can point you in the right direction, but after that it is up to you to solve the mystery, to find them, and to bring them back."

Okay where do we start?

"That is our question to you Ned. But first you should know that it will involve further travel and that will count as one more of your twelve adventures ... February perhaps?"

Oh, I hadn't thought about that.

"Think about that then Ned. Think hard, and while you are thinking, come up with one of your famous plans."

***

"So what do you say Santa? Shall we do it? I mean, shall I go to the tropics?" Ned was asking in all excitement.

"It's too risky Ned. I can't send you into possible danger like that."

They were gathered in Santa's study about the fireplace again sipping hot drinks, nibbling cookies. Ned had told those gathered in the room a little about his adventures with the Rhyll, as he showed them his crystalline friends. Five in all sat about listening in rapt concentration. Now they had arrived at the discussion phase in which they pondered the wisdom of Ned's half-formed plan. There was Santa, Crispin and Neville of course, also King Eirlys, ruler of the ice-fairies.

"I have heard tell of some special pebbles from my cousins the fire-fairies Santa," King Eirlys was saying. "I wonder if they would be the same gems as your solar opals."

"The Rhyll gave me a vision of where we need to go your majesty," Ned said. "I saw a sunset in a very red sky, redder than I've ever seen in my life. There was an ocean with palm trees growing near the water. I saw an orange fairy riding a seabird I think."

"That would be it! Yes I am sure of it. Only fire-fairies glow orange. I could go along with Ned to reason with those fairies Santa ... perhaps discover the whereabouts of these opals," King Eirlys offered.

"I could go along," said Neville hopefully, "to keep them both from harm."

"I-I-I could go too," squeaked a nervous Crispin.

"No Crispin. You and I are needed here," Santa said to the elderly elf. "We must remain to prepare for the worst while we continue to hope for the best. I don't feel happy about sending a child on a mission like this. Unknown territory may hold unknown peril. Oh ..." he breathed, reflecting longer still. "We have no better plan, do we? I do like the idea of King Eirlys and Neville joining you Ned. King Eirlys is very clever, and Neville is the most trustworthy lad of my acquaintance – and the strongest. If you are all keen to go, then I will not stop you. What has your Rhyll to say about having travelling companions Ned?"

"That is acceptable," the Rhyll said, as Ned touched its vocals.

"It says, and I quote: '*that is acceptable*'," he translated, "They have a peculiar way of talking."

"Wonderful!" Neville exclaimed, rubbing his palms together in gleeful anticipation. "I'm going on a trip! I can't tell how you excited I am Ned."

"You might faint from the heat," King Eirlys sniffed. "I am glad that I have my wings to cool me as I do not look forward to the heat."

"Oh but I do!" Neville replied. "I look forward to anything new. Have you ever been to the tropics Ned?"

"No I haven't Neville. It does get almost as hot in summer at times where I live. And, I have been to my own country's ocean before. ... What pot will we take Rhyll?" Ned asked.

"The design on the pot never really mattered Ned. It was your heart that we were reading, to which we added a twist of our own."

"Right ... well ... I will choose a nice pot for you anyway." Then looking over at Neville struggling to pull a huge embroidered blue satchel with red shoulder straps through the greenhouse's narrow doorway, he giggled, "You've got too much stuff there Neville. We won't be away that long."

"You never know," Neville replied, defending the contents of his luggage, "what will come up."

"I am traveling light," said King Eirlys brusquely, as he flew over the threshold with nothing at all in tow, "What happens now?"

"Now ..." Ned replied, closing the door, "we turn around."

They walked out of the greenhouse right into jungle thicket. They had to fight their way through its heavy undergrowth of ferns, orchids, bromeliads, and anthuriums. Neville had shifted his satchel onto his back, as had Ned who carried in his pack a few bits of food, water, his flashlight, some rope, a towel and a new red pot for the Rhyll. King Eirlys flew above and a bit beyond suggesting a path to follow. In this way they soon came to a clearing, a very narrow beach in fact, by an ocean at sunset where the sky was aflame in hot colours.

They all stopped as if on cue, taking in the incredible vista which was as still as an artist's painting, except for the small stirrings of a creature or two. The horizon seemed a very long way off, with only a few rocks and tiny treed islands to mark it. There was a sailboat moored in the bay, a large fish leaping playfully from water to air. All these were caught in faint reflections in the setting sun, the exact image that the Rhyll had shown Ned in his vision.

The foreground was populated by all sorts of lazy, wondrous creatures. Monkeys climbed slowly about in the palm trees, annoying small elf-like creatures who lounged in hammocks hanging from the branches. A rustic dock made of roughened wood jutted out into the water lending easy access from the jungle floor straight down to the oceanfront. Overhead an orange fairy flew on a Red-tail seabird.

But the most astonishing detail of this tropical scene was what, or who, was standing on that rustic dock right next to the Rhyll. She must have been two heads taller than Neville with very long arms and legs. Her lengthy red hair was tied loosely back; she wore a thin bathing costume of deep green over her lithe frame. Standing alone, she stared out to sea.

Ned had been so distracted in wonder that he failed to notice the crisis unfold, until King Eirlys began screaming in panic. Neville had fallen down where he stood, lying senseless in the sand. At the shrieks of the fairy, the woman on the dock ran forward and knelt by the yeti's side. "It's heat stroke. We need to get him into the water instantly!" With that, she lifted him as if he were a child and raced down the dock. Then putting an unconscious Neville on the dock-edge, she dived into the water, swimming back to slide him in with her. It took Ned longer to respond, but when he saw what the woman was doing, he threw off his clothes down to his lochamour suit and dived in after her, scooping the cool sea-water about his friend's face.

Within minutes Neville had roused, was staring with those melting brown eyes of his into the woman's own lovely green ones. "Hellooooo," he said in his typical friendly way. "I'm Neville. This is my friend Ned."

The woman smiled and looked at him kindly, still floating him on the water in her strong arms, "I am Maren, a daughter of Capricorns."

"That's a lovely name – Maren – isn't that a lovely name Ned?"

"You have too much hair for the tropics. That is why you fainted," Maren told him.

"We come from the cold North Pole, Maren," Neville explained, "or at least I do. King Eirlys who is flying about in a tizzy also lives in the North. Ned comes from somewhere in between the north and the tropics, isn't it Ned?"

"Well Neville from the North we are going to have to heat-proof you, if you wish to stay any length of time," Maren told him.

***

"I feel positively breezy," Neville announced, still in great spirits after his entire body had been shaved by Maren and Ned using a very sharp oyster shell and some coconut oil. They had left hair on top of his head but the rest had been stripped away. The overall look was quite pink and a bit raw, as he sat in his first pair of swimming trunks on the beach. Neville wasn't complaining. In fact he seemed to be enjoying the sensation of sand filtering through his toes while he played with some shells he had collected along the shore. Every once in a while he would stop what he was doing and take a huge sniff of air, sighing contentedly. "How delicious it all smells Ned!"

They were sitting in a group at the water's edge with the exception of King Eirlys who had flown off to introduce himself to his fairy cousins. "You called yourself a 'daughter of Capricorns' I think," said Ned. "What does that mean?"

"I think you non-tropic people have called us Amazon women," she said. "We aren't of course. We may be of that same family, but we live in the Tropic of Capricorn. We live at the ocean, not in jungles. I am the only one of my race who still lives here, now that my mother has passed."

"I think you're lovely," Neville swooned, clearly smitten with their new companion who turned away in a blush.

She was lovely. Her skin was clear and caramel coloured; her lips were the colour of chocolate mixed with raspberries. She was clearly human, although Ned did wonder if she might also be related to titan-humans, the scarp-dwellers. He made a mental note to ask her more when he knew her better.

Just then King Eirlys landed on the sand beside them all excited. "I know about solar opals!" he cried, "They call them 'vulcan opals' here, because they mine them from sleeping volcanoes."

"Who mines them your majesty?" Ned asked.

"We do," said an orange glowing fairy that flew down to join King Eirlys next to the group. "We mine them ... We sell them for quite a price as well."

"Ah, this is Queen Incendia," King Eirlys introduced the new fairy. "She and her kind paint the sunsets and sunrises."

Another long fairy name, Ned thought to himself with a chuckle. It wasn't the first time he had observed that fairy names were often bigger than they were. Then aloud he said, "Thank you for coming Queen Incendia. When you say 'quite a price' just what do you mean?"

"How much do you have to spend?" Queen Incendia asked.

"Nothing at all, to be honest," he replied.

"Then that is how many vulcan opals you will get," she retorted, in the usual rudeness of a fairy.

By now Ned knew his way around fairies. "Hmmm, that's not what King Magupu told Santa when he gave him that first batch of stones. I think King Magupu was showing his gratitude to Santa for the years – and years – that Santa has delivered presents to children, elves – and fairies – in the tropics. Do you know King Magupu, Queen Incendia? Do you know about Santa? Do you celebrate Christmas?"

Queen Incendia's tiny fairy eyes were filling up. *I kind of hated to do it*, Ned thought to himself. *But fairies need reminding at times.*

"Alright, alright!" she cried. "But we don't have many in stock. It will take days to carry enough down from Radiant Crater."

"What if we helped?" asked Ned.

***

"You need to travel lightly Neville," Maren was saying. "You must leave most of these things here." 'Here' was a cavern at the crater's base that Maren called home. It was easily as big as Neville's ice cave, although the walls, floors and ceiling were made of volcanic rock. The space was outfitted with furniture made of sculpted stone, driftwood and wicker. There were only a few pieces of furniture, but each piece was cleverly used. A large stone and driftwood table, for instance, had a larder of food at one end and an eating area at the other. Small slabs of rock served for both chairs and end tables. Maren's bed was a hammock, hung between two enormous stalactites woven from thin tropical vines, much like the ones the elves used in their swings at the beach, although Maren's was much larger of course. She had two chair-swings bolted in the same way as her bed, one at the cave entrance, one mid-cave hovering over a small pool of blue-green water. Her decorations made creative use of all the plants and minerals at her disposal. The lights in the cave were the same solar opals that they were seeking, not enough for their purposes, however. It was a confirmation that they were on the right track though.

"You have a beautiful home Maren," Neville had gushed, as they first entered the cave. "Isn't it beautiful Ned?"

Ned was having a great deal of fun swinging in the hammock chair over the blue-green pool as he watched Neville with Maren. Neville, the largest creature at the North Pole, looked quite small next to the giant woman. He clearly adored her, could not take his eyes from her even as she was scolding him, as she did now at the size of the satchel he was planning to take. Ned continued to watch, giggling as Maren pulled Neville's possessions from his sack – books, chess set, animal skins, winter-hardy vegetables, a watering can, a trowel, and miles of rope! "Only the rope is useful Neville, and the empty satchel for the opals. Please leave the rest here."

Maren had insisted that she come with them in search of the gems. She knew the route better than the fairies, she claimed. The fairies could fly to the top of the crater, they could not. Maren would take them most of the way through the tunnels which led from her cave. Only the last leg of their journey would be over the rough rocks on the outer edge of the crater. As planned, King Eirlys and Queen Incendia would meet up with them at the outer edge near the top in a few hours' time to help them in their final leg of the journey. Before their rendezvous the fairies would search out the best mine locations with the most opals for the taking.

Would you like to come Rhyll? Ned asked as he clutched its red pot. *Or would you be happier here?*

"We would feel pleasure to come with you Ned. We could offer advice. The final decisions, however, must be those agreed upon by you and your friends."

Great! I always like to have you around in any case. I think I will make some peanut butter on crackers for a snack before we climb, what do you think?

"We think that is a good idea Ned. Food is something that you biological creatures need for energy. Take some water along for the trip. Leave all but your rope, your flashlight and your Indigo here, to lighten your knapsack. We will travel in your bag. It has always been relatively comfortable for us."

Neville loved the peanut butter treats that Ned had prepared. "They are so delicious Ned ... aren't they delicious Maren!" he enthused.

Maren chose the tunnel at the far end of her cavern to begin their ascent. She had tied solar opals to the end of two sticks for herself and Neville, while Ned made use of his flashlight. She deftly steered them through a dark maze of narrow tunnels some of which even Ned had to stoop a little to get through. Maren and Neville had to take them on all fours. As they moved through the passages they were climbing as well, sometimes very steeply. At times they needed the help of their ropes, or Ned and Neville did in any case. Maren seemed to be able to climb very easily. She would throw a rope down to them when she reached a certain height to pull each up in turn.

In this way they made good progress through Radiant Crater. In just three hours Maren had led them to an opening in the rock beyond which they could once again smell fresh air. Only then did they stop their journey, sit and sip from their jars of water. After they had rested themselves Maren turned to Neville, "Could you open your satchel for me please Neville? I packed something in there with which to summon the fairies, to let them know where we are."

Maren retrieved a conch from Neville's sack which she brought to her lips and blew. A long hoot like a foghorn cut the stillness. She waited a few minutes before sounding again then returned the conch to the bag. "That should do, one blast to alert them, a second to bring them right to us."

King Eirlys and Queen Incendia landed almost before the conch could be put away. "We have found a good number of vulcan opals a bit larger than we usually take," Queen Incendia explained. "We would think this size too large to carry for a fairy, but they would be an easy load for you larger folks. There are hundreds to chose from, so you should have no trouble harvesting enough to do you a very long time. We can collect even more to allow the ice-fairies to have some for their homes as well," she added, giving King Eirlys a nod and a wink.

With this promise of success they continued their ascent on the outside of the crater this time. The rock-face was much steeper here; even Maren had difficulty with the climb. For the more sheer walls she asked the fairies advice on where to toss the looped end of a very long piece of rope to secure their guideline. Then she would haul herself up first, pulling the others up next. Although neither Neville nor Ned had ever climbed this far and this high before, they surprised themselves at how well they could manage without too many scrapes from the jagged rocks.

Another three hours brought them to a flat rock platform at the top of the crater. They stood for a brief time looking down into its steaming gap. "Are you sure it's extinct?" Ned asked Queen Incendia.

"For as long as I have been alive," she assured him, "and it certainly would be rude of you to ask me how long that is!"

As a rule when Ned got into the action stage of one of his plans, his daring spirit tended to kick in as his fears and anxieties took a back pew. If there was one exception to this rule, however, it would be very narrow paths along really tall mountains. So when Maren made them wear ropes about their waists at this point, he felt more than a little relieved. They followed the path along the edge of the crater in the direction that the fairies were constantly pointing. At times the ridge was so restricted that they had to slide along sideways, gripping at the sharp rocks to keep their balance. The fairies kept urging them forward, promising that the gems were within easy reach.

It was not an 'easy reach' as it turned out. The impossible path they had been following suddenly became impassible as it came to an end. "The opals are just there!" said Queen Incendia pointing a frustrated finger into the air, failing to see their dilemma.

'There' turned out to be on the far side of a gap between the path they were on and a ledge crowded with opal-encrusted stones. The ledge was well beyond their reach; the drop was sudden and deadly.

"Whoops," said Neville.

"Oh no," sighed Maren.

"Crap," muttered Ned. He opened his bag and pulled out the Rhyll. *Now what do we do*? he asked, feeling defeat for the first time.

"Think of where we have been with you before Ned. Think of what you have seen. Does nothing come to that clever mind?"

Ned crouched down as far from the edge of the ridge as possible with Neville beside him cheering him on. "You can figure this out Ned. I could too if I only had my encyclopedias with me. I knew I should have brought them ... Maren thought only the rope would be useful."

"That's it!" Ned cried, "That's the answer. Thank you Neville!"

"Most welcome ... what's the answer Ned?"

"How much rope do we have?"

***

"What's this that we've made Ned?" Neville asked, with a scratch to his forehead.

"It's a rope bridge Neville, or nearly one. I think it will do just the same."

With the help of all the members of the expedition Ned had designed and built a rope bridge like those of the scarp-dwellers, only without the wooden slats. It consisted of tightly-wrapped heavy rope, two strung across the gap for the feet, another two strung above these at hand height. King Eirlys and Queen Incendia wrapped the ropes around strong boulders at the far end while Neville and Maren tied them off at the other. Maren was attempting the crossing first.

"I have to confess I'm a bit nervous Ned," said Neville, watching Maren gracefully make her way. "There are no mountains like this at the pole. I've never tried to balance before, except on ice."

"Then imagine yourself on ice Neville. Slide your feet along the lower ropes, while you balance yourself with the upper ones."

Maren had reached the ledge and was urging them across. "It works very well. If it will hold me, you two should have no problem," she said in a light tone.

Ned made sure his knapsack was secured on his back before he placed one foot on the rope. He encouraged himself with an internal pep-talk, "Remember that rickety ladder at that nasty cliff on that foggy night at the lighthouse? This is shorter than that one. Remember that rope ladder you climbed to the skylight when you had to slide down just one rope into that terrible woman's house? This is less scary than that." He used these words to occupy his thoughts as he carefully slid his feet along the thick ropes holding tightly to the railings. He was on the ledge before he had even finished his self-encouraging speech, Maren thumping him roundly on the back.

Now Neville was crossing and muttering, "I'm sliding ... on ice ... I'm sliding ... on ice." At the halfway point, however, Neville's nerves took hold. He began to shake, so did the ropes. Maren and Ned held themselves very still not daring to startle him further. Neville regained control in short order looking to the sky, taking a cleansing breath, calming his legs, waiting for the ropes to stop quivering. Then he continued to move forwards, "I'm sliding ... on ice." He did slide wonkily over to them at last. Maren hugged the stuffing out of him when he reached solid rock, crying, "Oh, you had me so worried! Please don't scare me like that again."

They began picking up opals embedded in stones, or at least Neville and Maren did. The fairies pointed out the best ones that they had pre-selected. Ned placed most of them into Neville's sack with a few smaller ones into his own counting as he did until they had harvested about a hundred. "Is that enough do you think Neville?" he asked.

"Oh yes," Neville said, "Enough and then some."

Maren had just begun to cross the rope bridge for their return journey when the rumble began. She stopped, holding tight to the rope to keep herself safe until the first of the quaking had ceased. Then she retraced her steps to join Ned and Neville again on the ledge. King Eirlys and Queen Incendia bobbed and whooshed around their shoulders shrieking in panic.

Another rumble, another quake. Maren pointed towards the abyss. Hundreds of metres below, slowly rising, was a hot orange molten bubbling mass of lava. The next quake shuddered so forcefully that Ned was knocked off balance. As he tried to right himself, his left foot slipped on some loose gems toppling him from the shelf. Neville grabbed for one arm as he fell and held on tight, Ned swinging over the open fire pot. His knapsack had come loose from his shoulders. He struggled to hold onto it and onto Neville as well, who was beginning to slide towards the edge himself ... Which is when Neville shouted down to him, "Let the bag go Ned! You can't lose your life for a knapsack of trinkets."

... and he shouted back, "You know it's more than that, much more... The Rhyll – it's in my backpack. I will not let it go for anything."

An arm reached over Neville's shoulder just then to steady him. It was Maren, in rescue mode. "You just concentrate on holding Ned. I will pull you both back." She braced her feet against a boulder, both arms around the widest part of Neville's shoulders straining against his weight, Ned's – and gravity. But she was a daughter of Capricorns. She had strength even beyond her own estimation. She hauled them both up as one, yanking them far back from the edge.

"We must act quickly," she barked, taking control. "No time to lose! Get over the bridge as quickly as you can." She grabbed Ned's bag from him and slung it over her own shoulders. "Neville, make sure that your satchel is balanced first. Go! I will follow." It was all done very hastily. As they were in too much of a hurry to even think about doubts or panic, they had soon re-crossed the bridge.

On the other side now, Maren's clear instructions continued. "We must leave this bridge; no time to take it down. I just hope that we have enough rope for our descent."

"I brought lots Maren don't you fret," Neville piped up.

The fairies were still spinning over the gap chaotically prompting Ned to observe to Maren, "I know some creatures whose wings were burned away by fire."

"Yes," Maren agreed, as she got the fairies' attention. "Move away from the gap, far away. But, do meet us by the rock platform, for we must climb back down very quickly."

They retraced the ridge path to their descent point where the fairies were hovering in wait. Maren looped one end of their rope around a boulder, tossing the rest over the edge before she shimmied down. Then she held it tightly, as Ned and Neville slid down in turn. "Would one of your majesties please loosen the loop?" she called up. When Maren had the loop again in hand she placed it around another strong piece of rock, the descent continuing. By the third looping and re-looping, the fairies had regained control of their fears allowing the process to quicken, making it possible for them to reach the upper tunnel opening safely and without further fuss or distraction.

Here Maren addressed the team again. "This event might be anything from a volcanic burp to a full-scale eruption. I have no idea what we will find in the tunnels. We have no choice though; we must use them to get down."

She led them back through the tunnels more quickly than they had climbed up just hours before. As they ran over the rough rock, they could feel the air heating behind them as the lava pursued. On two occasions she stopped their progress to have Neville assist her in blocking the passage they had just come along. As the second boulder had been shoved into place they could see a red glow through the cracks and realized that although they had slowed it, the lava was following them nonetheless. But the boulders were giving them time, perhaps just enough. At the base of the crater they ran into Maren's cavern and began stripping it of all furniture and supplies, taking them well into the jungle. Maren and Neville together were a well-oiled machine, hauling unimaginably heavy loads between them. Even so at their last load they clearly saw the ooze of hot rock as it seeped in at her back door.

While Maren, Neville and Ned did the lifting, the fairies scoured the beach and jungle floor to warn any creatures living in the path of the crater of the danger. When all creatures and home contents had been secured, they returned to the beach to wait and watch. They stayed there for hours witnessing a rising of steam with no lava spilling over the top yet. "We may be okay this time," Maren announced to her neighbours, "but we will need to wait longer to be sure. We must study the crater more fully before we trust it again. It was fortunate that we had early warning, very lucky that we saw the lava when we did. If we hadn't gone up to the mines today, things might have gone much worse for us all."

***

"I'm staying in the South," Neville told Ned, as they packed the solar opals into the greenhouse.

"Are you sure Neville?" Somehow he wasn't surprised to hear it. "Are you very sure?"

"More sure than I have ever been of anything Ned. I have lived in a wonderful home, in a magical place called North Pole Pax Inc. I have had loyal friends who were kind and nice enough to say that they liked my vegetables. Even with all of this, I've been lonely. I was the only yeti you see, no chance of a family. But here in this place, even though it has only been a few hours, I know I fit in. I fit in – with Maren. She's lovely! Don't you think she's lovely Ned? She thinks I'm lovely too. She feels like family to me already. Then there's her home to replace ..."

"What about the heat, Neville? You fainted from the heat."

"Oh I'll get used to the heat even if I have to shave every bit of my body every day! Ask Santa to bring me a nice razor next Christmas will you Ned?"

King Eirlys patted Neville on the shoulder and flew into the greenhouse to wait. Meantime, Neville had reached his hand into his satchel to retrieve a crude box he had made of palm leaves, placing it in Ned's hands. "I want you to have this Ned. I need you to remember me."

Ned peeled back the wrapping to reveal Neville's father's well-worn copy of *Robinson Crusoe.* "This must the best present I ever received Neville," Ned blubbed, his throat starting to swell with emotion. Then he dashed into the greenhouse, returning moments later with the red flower pot in which he had placed all of his leftover vegetable seeds. "I want you to have these," he said. "I need you to remember me too Neville. ... Oh one more thing – very important," he added, pulling his pouch from around his neck and selecting one of his three diamonds. "This is a growing stone for the many gardens that I know you will plant wherever you are. It will make everything you grow as tall as you are."

Neville squeezed Ned into a huge bear hug, whispering through sniffles, "Imagine the adventures Maren and I are going to have Ned ... Just imagine."

Chapter Ten:
Earth-Rise

When he arrived back at the North Pole with the opals and King Eirlys, Ned had been of two minds. He was excited at the load of gems that he and the fairy king would present to the big man; he looked forward to telling their tale. But he dragged his feet at his sad duty of informing them about Neville's decision to stay. Having said goodbye to so many friends himself, he had some idea about the regret they would feel.

It was Crispin who was the most inconsolable. Big tears rolled over those ruddy cheeks and down into his collar. "How could Neville leave us like this?" he wailed, "What will we do without him?"

"How could he *not* leave us Crispin?" Santa counselled, "Neville has realized his fondest wish ... and he has found his heart."

Before their final parting Santa took Ned aside in his study out of earshot of the others. "You have done well Ned. You have saved us all from great hardship. More than that, you have been a good friend, to our dear Neville especially."

"I will miss him more than I can say," Ned confessed.

"As will I," Santa agreed, "Now sadly you and your Rhyll must also leave. Before you do, let me give you some solar opals from those you harvested. I have a feeling that some day you will put them to good use." He laid five small liquid-white gems into Ned's hand the energy of which extended beyond his palm, infusing him with warmth and enduring memories.

As he returned to his garden Ned skipped about in the snow, heart overflowing, "Whatever could top this adventure Rhyll? ... Unless we go to moon!"

***

In September of that same year Ned and the Rhyll went to the moon.

"Whoops," he blurted involuntarily, as he stepped from the greenhouse into the biosphere. *I'm indoors ... so is the greenhouse.*

The structure was vast in size, so vast that Ned could not see a beginning or an end to it. Its rounded ceiling and walls were made entirely of thick glass panels, held in place by a strong lattice of galvanized steel. Inside this massive dome were smaller buildings stacked one on top of another, similar in concept to the scarp-dwellers' but not quite so higgledy-piggledy. In this weather-controlled environment, these buildings were lightly constructed of wood and glass with ornate brass fittings. Cast-iron spiral staircases led from floor to floor.

Plants were everywhere, some in pots around the buildings, also in masses of flats placed in the open spaces. There were huge specimens of flowers, shrubs, and vegetables growing on tables higher than those in Neville's North Pole greenhouse. The tables were stacked on top of each other to maximize the growing space. At the far end of the plant stacks stood an enormous water tank made of brass, with a giant spigot dripping water into a long deep trough. The floor was smooth concrete well-brushed in some areas, straw-covered in others. Two goats roamed about in the straw, nibbling away at anything leafy within reach of their teeth.

Between the plant stacks and the buildings, an enormous telescope shared space on a high trolley with a middle-aged man and young woman. The heavenly body they were studying through the lens – none other than Earth!

Seeing the familiar markings of his own planet looming on the horizon jarred Ned into recalling his excited comment to the Rhyll in the thrill of a moment some months before. *The Rhyll took me at my word. Here we are ... moon-side! Exciting.... now what?*

Ned had gotten adept at not being seen, though he knew he must make himself known before long. The best way he figured was a straight-forward approach and the best starting place just might be that telescope stand. At the very least he was concerned that his popping out of nowhere would startle the astronomers. At the very most he feared that his presence would cause them to panic, that he would be identified as an illegal on the station, and that security staff would jump him, pitching him from the biosphere.

What actually happened was bizarre, almost comical. Perhaps it was because he had made his greeting sound casual. In any case the young woman on the platform was neither startled nor fearful. Her reaction was one of near indifference. She was so engaged in her duties, in fact, that she took a couple of beats before even turning her head.

"Oh you must have come in with the new supply shuttle. It's a bit early ..." She jumped down from trolley to platform, from platform to floor, sprinted up to him and held out a brusque but welcoming hand. She was quite young, perhaps no more than six to eight years older than he, although he was rubbish at guessing such things. She stood one head taller, though she was slighter in build. She was dressed simply in a uniform – a jumpsuit of navy blue with an insignia of a moon overlapping an image of Earth, like two interlocking wedding rings, with the letters "LBP" above the logo, "SCIENTIST" beneath. Her pale face was evenly featured without a trace of makeup. The straight brown hair cascading down her back could have used a detangle and a good trim.

"Dr. Mercy Applegate, Director of the Lunar Bio-dome Project, West Sector ... at your service," she said, in a no-nonsense voice.

"Ned, student, from Earth ... at yours."

"Are you with one of the shuttle pilots, or are you part of the relief team?"

"Neither really ..." he confessed honestly. He was thinking about how to explain this further, but she had already moved off the question.

"Shall we put you to work? All hands on deck so to speak while you're here? What are your interests ... skills?"

"I'm good at science at school – botany, well gardening ... and astronomy."

"Home-schooled of course, as per the *Moon Pact;* reached Level Four of the program I suppose? I do wish they would let us know in advance about these work placements. Well we don't pay as you know. However, we will educate you through work experience, provide your meals, give you a room in one of the units. What's your first choice? The Biology Sector? Botany? Astronomy? Geology? Physics? Dome Maintenance? Perhaps the Artificial Gravity Division? Or shall we just start you on general duties in all of them and allow you to choose after a few days?"

"I-I-I ..." Ned began.

"My brother Oliver will show you the ropes. Oliver! Over here will you? Oliver, this is Red."

"Ned."

"Right. Ted. Show him the ropes, get him a bunk," she shouted, as she whooshed away.

"Ned is it?" asked the young man.

"That's right. I got a bit confused myself for a moment there," Ned returned.

"Right, well that's Mercy for you; always in a rush; never listens much. I think she gets a bit defensive because she is young to be in the job she's in. She's brilliant at what she does – no one better."

Oliver was a rather plain-looking young man a few years senior to Ned, not much taller but a few pounds heavier. His dirty-blonde hair was slicked back and he too wore a uniform. His jumpsuit was deep green, however, with the same logo as his sister's, except instead of "SCIENTIST" underneath it said "ASSISTANT". It took no time for Ned to conclude that Oliver was much more relaxed than his sister.

"Shall we get you digs first?" Oliver suggested. "Where's your kit?"

"I don't really need all that," Ned replied nervously. "I won't be here long and I already have a place to stay."

"Right – tour then?"

"I'd like that very much."

"Let's go indoors first," said Oliver, "I have a feeling we're going to get wet anytime now." A gentle ping sounded; Oliver yanked Ned's arm, directing him under the cover of a building. An old man dozing in a deck chair near the housing units suddenly wakened, taking his folding chair with him; the astronomers covered their telescope and jumped from the platform immediately. All took cover with Ned and Oliver under the houses.

In the next minute it started to rain, an even shower of medium strength lasting about five minutes, just long enough to thoroughly wet all the vegetation. The spray seemed to descend from small openings in the steel grid-work. The goats were gleeful as they kicked about lapping the water from the floor. Just as suddenly, it stopped. Next Ned heard the faint hum of fans sucking away the heavy mist from the air. This lasted an additional three minutes, then everyone returned to their duties or leisure. "You'll need to watch the clock for the daily deluge," Oliver remarked, "or carry a big umbrella," he added with a smirk.

First on their tour was the indoor astronomy lab with all its bells and whistles. "We've been on the moon a while as you know," Oliver explained, "Much longer than humanity would ever expect, nearly a hundred years. That's why the decor is Victorian funky.

We've kept up with the technology, however, all that is state-of-the-art. It's just the buildings and twiddly bits that are old. Nothing wears out under the dome."

"I have no idea what any of this is," Ned exclaimed in rapt fascination looking at the clutter of technology. "It sure looks awesome though. How far can you see into space?"

"As much as fifteen billion light years away, or so I'm told," said Oliver, "That's Mercy's specialty not mine."

"Wow!" Ned exclaimed, "when I get home I'm going to look up what that means."

"Well when you do, you just may see photos like these," Oliver explained as he pulled up some images onto a giant monitor. Ned lost himself completely in the images – vivid splashes of colour against a dense black background, swirls, rings, all manner of patterns, all resembling "join-the-dots" puzzles where the dots were a myriad of stars. He only wrenched his eyes from the screens when Oliver suggested that he might like to see, maybe use, their most powerful telescope himself.

***

"What you're seeing there is Venus, Ted," said Mercy, as she adjusted the focus. "I've put on a filter that allows you to see the blue behind all those clouds." Then turning the scope in another direction and refocusing she showed him another wonder. "This is Saturn. I've turned on the infrared so you can see all the textures and densities of the planet, its rings, its moons."

"I'm definitely going to be learning a lot more about Saturn," Ned enthused. "This astronomy stuff is very exciting Dr. Applegate!"

"It really is. That's just within our solar system Red. I haven't even shown you the Extreme Deep Fields!" Mercy sighed, looking relaxed as she stared into the Earth-light.

***

"Just how many animals do you have here on the moon Oliver?" Ned asked as he wandered around South Sector now with the young assistant.

"We keep the population quite low Ned. Otherwise there would be more animals than humans in no time. A few cows and goats provide us with dairy products like milk, cheese and butter. Those are the largest animals so far on the moon. We also keep a dozen chickens, just for the eggs. It's easier to be vegetarian on the moon Ned. The few things we can't grow for ourselves come on the shuttles about every four months.

"We're allowed to have pets for companionship, but we also study them in the same way as we are studying ourselves. We are still looking at the effect that being in space has on various species. We've had dogs, cats, mice, gerbils and hamsters. No other farm animals so far, birds or wild animals ... although East Sector does study fish and insects. It's amazing that, even after a hundred years, we've only just begun."

"Ah! The Gardens! That's what I'm training for. I want to be Chief Botanist some day," Oliver was proclaiming as they entered an area dedicated entirely to the growing and nurturing of plants. Ned was amazed at the sheer size of them. There were species of flowers, vegetables and fruit that were bigger here than any Ned had ever seen on Earth. "We grow stuff everywhere in the biosphere, anywhere we have extra space, but these are our main gardens. Besides growing all this as food for ourselves, we also study how well plants grow and adapt in space. The moon is a good place to start. Moon days and nights here are different than you have on Earth. We get two weeks of daylight followed by two weeks of night, all year long. The sunlight is much harsher up here as well; those glass panels you see have filters for reducing the strength and severity of the sun's rays. Most of the plants have adjusted well, some better than others as you see. They can grow much larger than they do on Earth, for reasons we still can't explain."

***

Ned was scratching the ear of a red cocker spaniel that was covering him in welcoming licks. "What do you think of us so far, Ted?" Mercy asked as she bolted her food. "Oops ...late ... must dash." She was off again leaving Ned, Oliver and dog to finish off their lunches at the only table in the tiny apartment.

The apartment shared by brother and sister was located in West Sector next to the Mercy's astronomy lab and platform. The three closet-sized rooms were simply set up. The two bedrooms were identically furnished except for the dog bed in Oliver's room. There were mattresses, light sheets, blankets and thin pillows all placed on a plain wooden floor. Table lamps rested on the floor next to the beds in each room, books were stacked in high piles in the remaining free space. In the main living area was a galley kitchen, a basic dining area, two computer work stations, all nearly obscured by books and papers. The only objects of interest in the entire apartment in fact were enormous chunks of luminous pinkish-white crystals which added a certain brightness to an otherwise boring space. As with all moon apartments this one had no bathroom. Everyone was expected use one of four common buildings fitted with toilets and showers located in each of the sectors.

"I have a really great question," Ned said, mid-mouthful of a rather dull sandwich. He washed it down with plain water before going on. "My great question is this ... How do you keep from floating up to the ceiling, you know with the moon having less gravity?"

"That's what made moon living possible in the first place Ned. A man by the name of Arthurs, Dr. C. K. Arthurs, discovered these minerals up here that are just wizard. You see them lying about our rooms? Well they're everywhere throughout the biosphere really. Dr. Arthurs found that the crystals had these abilities, like enormous power, energy of course, but more than just that. Anyway he reckoned the crystals themselves must have inspired him to design these amazing gravity stabilizers. Since then we've been on the moon."

"How come no one knows you're here? I mean how could this be kept a secret for more than a hundred years?"

"That was the other great thing that Dr. Arthurs thought up. He figured it was going to be really hard to keep the secret, so he made it a rule right at the outset that the moon project would be 'family only'. There were five families chosen to be involved in the project; only members of those five families have ever lived or worked here. All the generations of children in those families were either born on the moon or were trained from the start in the moon business, knowing the importance of its secrecy. It solves all sorts of other issues as well, security for one.

"We had to tell the biggest governments on Earth of course, once they began inventing their own smart telescopes. So far we've been able to fob them off with promises to share anything we find. As far as regular folks knowing? The dome is kind of camouflaged you see. You can't see it with ordinary telescopes unless you're really looking hard. There have been rumours of course ... But no big breaches yet, 'fingers crossed'. Which family are you from by the way?"

"The Irish one," said Ned, 'fingers crossed' under the table.

"Thought so," Oliver replied, and Ned started breathing again.

They had gone to North Sector after their meal. Oliver had asked the scientist in charge to show Ned the really long core samples they'd recently taken by drilling far beneath the moon's surface. "We're looking for minerals that we just might need down on Earth," the woman explained. "At the rate we're using up our resources down there, the sooner we develop new ones, the better."

A loudspeaker crashed in to steal away the moment, "Battle Stations, West Sector, Battle Stations! This is not a drill, I repeat ..."

"What's wrong?" Ned shouted to Oliver as he raced far ahead of him towards West Sector like his pants were ablaze.

Chapter Ten

"We got ants!" he shouted back, not missing a beat.

⁂

"Okay, we can't use conventional weaponry in the biosphere," Oliver was explaining to Ned as he thrust a stun gun into his hand. "Any kind of explosion or bullet could damage the dome, then we'd all be sunk. When the ants get anywhere close to you zap 'em with one of these. I'm going to join the guys with the water cannons. We reckon if we can get the ants off their feet they won't be able get back up, then we've got 'em. We've only seen them from a distance up to now, in the subterranean tunnels ... so we're kind of guessing a bit here."

"If they're ants, how about ant traps or sugar in a bottle, you know something a bit less violent?"

"You haven't seen how big these suckers are Ned. Anyway they're not real ants, they're robotic."

Ned stood there alone with his mouth agape watching Oliver join a team of twenty men, women and children in various coloured jumpsuits that were forming a line behind six water cannons. "Well, I'm not shooting anyone, stun gun or not," he shouted out to Oliver from his position behind a potted evergreen.

Mercy rushed over to hurry along the old man from the deck chair, "Grandpa, either you stay here with me, or join the medics in the rear."

"I'm with you girly. Let's not forget who's in charge here!"

There were several teams of 'jumpsuits' at the ready. Besides the water cannon crew, some had iron javelin-like rods, long kitchen knives and thick pieces of timber. They were scientists not soldiers but everyone stood at the ready. At least fifty colonists in Ned's estimation stood staunchly prepared for battle, with ten more in the background holding stretchers and packs of medical supplies. They were waiting for something robotic to come forth from a large hatch just south of the astronomy platform.

They came.

When the first one poked a long antenna up from the hatch, it was blasted by a stream of water, causing it to fall back into the hole. This foil only delayed the action by a minute or so. The next time it appeared it burst forth quickly, being shoved forward by its comrades from the rear.

They were the oddest anything that Ned had ever seen. In fact if he didn't know differently, he'd have said they were man-made, maybe even child-made. Their legs and antennae were made of cast iron shapes and brass gears. Every inch of them seemed metallic, a bit like Dad's old Meccano set pieces with multiple joints and weird shapes. Perhaps what made them dangerous was their sheer size, fifteen to twenty metres high, walking awkwardly on the shiny concrete surfaces.

One 'ant' already felled by a water cannon, had turned upside down, its limbs writhing hopelessly as it tried to right itself. It was replaced in line by a larger robotic, more like a spider than an ant. The 'spider', more agile, was not deterred by the water blasts. It focused on the group of colonists with stun guns which were proving useless at stopping it from stepping over their bodies on its way to the astrology lab where it pounded away at the walls.

Medics were rushing in with stretchers all the while, lifting injured workers, transporting them to North Sector where a makeshift infirmary had been set up in one of the common buildings.

When Mercy saw the robotic spider crushing her lab, she charged at it using her only weapon, a two metre long rod with which she tried to unbalance it. She was joined by her Grandpa who hacked away at the legs with a long knife. After several smacks at one particular lower leg joint, the spider began to wobble. Realizing that she was gaining advantage, Mercy kept hacking away until it toppled like a felled tree right on top of Grandpa, pinning him down under its cast iron abdomen.

From his position of cover Ned had been watching the confusion, not knowing where, how, or if he fit in. He could not understand what he was seeing, could not reason why there should be anything robotic under the moon's crust, let alone why they were in combat with them. When he saw the old man fall, saw Mercy rush to him, trying to free him, he dropped the stun gun and raced to assist.

"Just leave me girly," the old guy was gasping. "I'm a goner anyway."

"No you're not!" Ned and Mercy shouted together. Ned called out to Oliver, "Over here man ... bring a few other guys with you!"

It took five of them to lift the abdomen enough, one more to slide the old man free. He was alive but unable to walk, breathless as well. Two medics came up, slung Grandpa onto a stretcher and whisked him away immediately. Not stopping to draw breath, Ned, Mercy and Oliver joined members of the other teams who were fending off two remaining ants that were still upright pushing forward despite the efforts of the colonists' defence lines.

"Where's your stun gun?" Oliver shouted at Ned as they approached one of the two remaining ants.

"I told you I'm not using it. I'm fourteen years old for goodness sake. I'm no soldier, neither are you."

Then true to form Ned got a plan. He raced off to the greenhouse, grabbed his rope, and returned before any of them had noticed him gone.

"I think we can take them both down at once," Ned shouted to Oliver.

"What?" Oliver returned, trying to aim his cannon. "What are you doing with that rope?"

"Just grab hold of an end. We'll make a trip line. They seem to want to attack buildings more than people. I think we can predict which way they'll be heading. Trust me I'm good with ropes."

He sprinted over to the water tower, tying his end of the rope to its broad base, while Oliver pulled the other end over to one of the thick supporting beams for the roof. The two ants advanced together. Their antennae were directed towards the buildings, not watching the ground so when they fell together it took them completely unawares. While Oliver raced back to his place for more rope, Ned watched as the mechanical insects flailed their limbs trying to recover their balance. Then the two young men dodged and weaved as they attached rope to one leg of each creature, wrapping it around many times until all the legs were stilled.

***

Ned was sifting through the wreckage of the half-dozen robotics trying to make sense of the carnage. By now the colonists were doing their clean-up and the wounded were returning home. There had been no loss of human life thank goodness, although Grandpa was not doing well.

The 'spider' was in pieces as were three of the ants. The two that Ned and Oliver had tripped and bound with rope were still intact. Ned was most interested in the fragments, however, more than in their robotic hostages. Two of the broken 'ants' had fractured skulls. When Ned examined the skull remains he found fragments of the pinky-white crystals inside, just like the ones that he had seen earlier in the Applegate apartment. Most of them were smashed into bits while others were mildly damaged.

Are these crystals what power the robots? he mused to himself, *or what drives them?*

"Precisely."

What? Who?

"Rhyll here."

In my head? Rhyll in my head?

"It was always our goal Ned. To commune with you telepathically."

Job done! Where are you?

"We are in a dark tunnel just under your feet. There is something that you must see."

You won't just zap yourself back up here? You know ... as we both know you can do?

"No Ned, you must not ignore the tunnels."

Oh crap, I mean okay. I'll find a way.

The hatchway that had been forced by the robots seemed the most logical underground access. Ned waited patiently, slowly inching his way closer, and when he was fairly certain that he wasn't being watched, he slipped into the dimly-lit hole. The staircase downward was badly damaged by the metal beasts, but it was still passable with Ned holding tightly to the railings to get over the rougher bits. When he reached the next level down he discovered an engine room with big brass tanks, strange gauges and wires, all connecting with the level above. Perhaps this room controlled the power or plumbing for the dome. Ned could not stop to reason this out, however, because this was not where he needed to be. Where he needed to be, he reckoned, was through that giant hole in the wall. By the looks of it, it had been recently made. Actually by the looks of it, it had been patched and re-patched several times.

Ned climbed a tall pile of rubble to the dark entranceway into a great unknown beyond. He wished he had been organized enough to bring light. As it turned out he could see quite well by the glow of the crystalline ceiling. Never had he seen such a spectacle of natural crystals. Except of course for the Rhyll...

"Ned?"

Yes Rhyll?

"Well done."

Shall I pick you up?

"Not yet. Look about you first and tell us what you see."

I see crystals, very bright and beautiful, more here than I've ever seen on Earth.

"Yes, and what do you know about them?"

They remind me a bit of you; they glow in the dark ... There's maybe a bit more I know. Oliver, a great guy I met, was telling me that they use these crystals to power their technology. He said something else that kind of made me wonder ...

"Which is ..."

Which is that the first scientist who invented the gravity stabilizer said he must have been inspired by these crystals. That was his word – 'inspired' ...

"And ..."

And I just was looking at the wreckage of the robotic insects and I saw some of these crystals inside their heads. I was wondering if the crystals were powering the robots, or ...

"Or ..."

Or if they were driving them.

"Impressive. You are not only hearing better but you are observing better as well."

And I'm much taller now. Have you noticed?

"Just so. What you are saying then is that you think these crystals are intelligent."

That's what I was beginning to think, yes.

"If they have intelligence then ..."

Then they are a life form. And maybe they belong here ... and just maybe we don't.

"There is much to be learned in any case."

How? It took me a long time to understand you...

"You will negotiate ... We will translate."

***

"Oliver," Ned said to his new friend, "Can you keep an open mind?"

"I'd like to think of myself as an explorer Ned. And to be an explorer, you need an open mind."

"Remember you said that when you see what I have to show you ... and keep it open wider still when you hear what I have to tell you."

Chapter Ten

***

"You can't call a meeting like this Oliver," Mercy stormed into the central meeting hall in a fit of pique. "Who said you could? Who made you the boss of me – of us!"

"I did," said the Dr. Hiram Applegate, Director and one of the earliest colonists of the biosphere, also known to Mercy and Oliver as 'Grandpa'. "The boy makes sense, so does his friend. In fact if you don't listen now, we'll be packing up and going home ... or worse," he added ominously.

"I'm going to let Ned start this off," Oliver was saying, "It was he that figured all this out. Well him and ..." Ned stopped him with a look that said, *Don't tell that bit!*

Ned stood in front of the crowd. It wasn't the first time he had addressed a group, and it never got any easier. "Would it surprise you to know that you are not alone on the moon?"

"If you mean that there's life on the moon, Red, then all I can say is that we would have come across life forms before now if there were. Except for those horrible ant thingies," Mercy quipped hotly. "Don't tell me those mechanical contraptions are worth having around after what they have done to us! I'd prefer studying their carcasses thank you very much."

"Who made the 'ants' and who controls them? What if there were living creatures inside them?" Ned replied.

"There aren't; we already looked."

"What if they were mineral-based?"

"Phooey," scoffed a geologist in the back of the room, "Minerals have energy, they do not have intelligence. They don't *know* that they're minerals."

"Yes they do," Oliver piped up, "I was sceptical as well, but I have talked with them."

The room of scientists all began to mutter at once. At this point Dr. Applegate the elder pulled himself up in his chair and spoke out again. "I knew Dr. C. K. Arthurs ..." The room quietened again

178

out of respect. "He was an old man when I was a boy. I was born in this biosphere as most of you know, and I will die here I expect." He took a sip of water and a sniff of pure oxygen from a tank by his side.

"As a boy, I had the honour working with our founder. I loved the man dearly, as a son would a father. I listened to him all the time, to the stories that most people ignored. Which is probably why he told me one particular story, told me only once mind, but I will never forget it. 'Hiram,' he said when we were alone one day in his lab, 'Everyone thinks I invented the gravity stabilizer. Would it surprise you to know that I did not?' And of course I said that it would surprise me very much. 'The design of the gravity stabilizer and many of my inventions I'm afraid – with the exception of the rocket propulsion unit that brought us here – all of them were the work of these pink and white crystals here. They speak to me, explain designs, show me details. They have been speaking to me all along. It is only with their assistance that I have guided the Lunar Bio-dome Project all my life.'

"I said nothing about what Arthurs told me even after he was gone. I didn't understand why he was telling me this story. Perhaps if I had we wouldn't be in this mess now. I thought that my idol had gone mad you see ... And now we have gone too far. Today I have understood my error all too well and you should know yours ... You should listen to Oliver and Ned. They have discovered the truth where I have failed to." Old Dr. Applegate slumped back in his chair placing the oxygen mask around his nose once more.

He nodded at Ned who moved forward again. "They call themselves Selenophites and you have been killing them. Did it not occur to you to ask how these robotic insects suddenly appeared on the moon? Didn't you wonder why they chose this moment to fight, after a hundred years?

"It was Dr. C. K. Arthurs himself who built the robotic insects, built them as tools for the Selenophites so that they could expand their underground world, dig more tunnels for new life to expand – their children so to speak. In return, they gave him the technological ideas to build the biosphere. Dr. Arthurs made a better world possible for them, a world that you are now destroying with your new deep-cutting drills. You have cut through into their world and damaged them – unintentionally of course. And today you have killed them outright by crushing them as they used their robots to get you to stop." He looked around at their grim, sad faces and sat down.

Now Oliver addressed the teams looking every inch the leader. "I don't know their language as well as Ned here, but he showed me how to begin. I saw things ... saw little sparks of molecules slowly growing in the new tunnels, saw them expand into crystals, saw crystals multiply into pods – pods that are centuries old and just as wise."

"We've been studying the effects that living on the moon might have on Earth lifeforms. When are we going to study the results of what Earth lifeforms have done to the moon?"

***

"Good speech," said Ned to Oliver as he picked up the Rhyll and hid it in the folds of his jacket, "I liked that last bit especially."

"How will I know what to do from here?" Oliver said, brows furrowing, "How will I know what they are saying without you and your Rhyll to translate?"

"If a C. K. Arthurs can learn Selen-tongue," Ned said with a smile, "so can an Oliver Applegate. We think you've got potential!"

"What family name was that – the Irish one?" Oliver asked with a grin. "Donahue right?"

"Clery ... Ned Clery."

<h1 style="text-align:center">Chapter Eleven:
Ned in The Future</h1>

"We're breaking up Ned," Maeve was shouting across the room on a sweltering July day the following year.

"I didn't know we were going out," he replied evenly. He was used to Maeve's outbursts by now.

"Well if we were, I'd be breaking up with you right now!" she replied, still keeping the heat in her tone.

Ned turned around in his desk-chair. He had been so absorbed by his new computer the whole morning, a birthday gift, while Maeve sat flipping through magazines on his bed. "But why? What have I done?"

"You're always at that stupid computer or with your nose in a book. Look man I'm as good a student as you, but I don't spend every waking moment studying anything and everything ... all the time ... ignoring my friends ... what I might have left of them anyhow. It's summer for goodness sake." Her speech lost both heat and momentum at the very end and she sat down on the floor in a pout.

Ned closed his computer. "You're right. I just get so curious, then I completely lose track of the time. What shall we do now? I'm always up for a swim," he said, grabbing for his trunks and towel.

Maeve sprung to her feet and threw her arms about his neck, "Now that's the guy I know and like."

"Besides my parents you're the only one who will tell me when I go off-key," he said, touching his forehead to hers, placing his arms lightly about her waist. "Thanks."

"Come on you screw-up," she giggled, kissing his cheek lightly.

***

"I prepared a nice pot for you Rhyll," Ned said as he sat next to it in his garden at the August full moon, just two weeks after he turned fifteen. "But I want you to choose where to go this time. You chose better than me."

"We have already selected your next 'adventure' as you call it," the Rhyll replied, "although we must communicate with you before we transport."

"Right. This is a first. No surprises this time? Fire away." Ned lay on his back on the lawn.

"Up to now we have taken you to places unknown."

"Cor-rect!"

"You have been helpful with situations and puzzles that you have encountered each time."

"Have I?"

"Yes."

"Good to know."

"But all these events have occurred more or less around the time in which you are living."

"I wondered about that."

"Just so. On this occasion, however, we have selected a journey far out of your time, well into your future in fact."

"Wow! That should be exciting."

"That is why we must talk first. There will be rules for this exercise."

"Exercise is it? So you're my teacher?"

"We like to think that we present opportunities for you to teach yourself. Our role is one of advisor."

"Great idea! Is it working?"

"Most assuredly. You also have been our teacher."

"How's that? What could I ever teach you?"

"You are teaching us about humanity. We have been studying the creatures of Earth for hundreds of years."

"So I'm your experiment?"

"Not quite. It is more that you are an example of the best of your species. In a few hundred more years, with sufficient data, we may feel confident enough to make ourselves known to more of earth-kind."

"Okay, I see how that works. Glad to help. What about the future? How is this different?"

"The future is not your timeline Ned; you must not change it. You may counsel those you meet in small ways. You may even enjoy their company. But you must not alter the timeline by your words or actions."

"No Ned plans then?"

"No Ned plans, as you say."

"Right. Got it. Off we go."

***

Ned could guess by the slope of the greenhouse that he would be stepping out onto uneven ground. It was both steep and rocky. He was up high. *Oh not this again*, he couldn't help but think, *we've done mountain cliffs. Been there* ... This one was different, however, this qualified as desolate. It was all rock and one lone tree. The air was so thin that he was seriously considering sucking on his Indigo for a bit to get over that woozy feeling.

This is the future?

The night sky was pitch black, no visible moon, no light except for the occasional bolt of lightning. It was only in these brief lightning displays that Ned could see any detail at all, could see what else perched on this cold mountain top along with him. The first indications of life were a few mountain goats sprinting about the sheer walls like their hooves were naturally sticky.

A jagged slash of lightning ripped through the dark air once more, this time striking something close by with a loud snap and a fountain of sparks. *What could that lightning have zapped up here that would cause fireworks like that*? Ned lay down on the rocks sticking his face just far enough over the edge to see what lay beyond. What he saw was a building suspended in air. Except for a couple of anchor points in the rock this structure hung on its own, dangling nowhere, touching nothing. What's more there was another one – same idea, different design – wedged between two narrow peaks farther off in the distance.

The idea of a hanging pod completely fascinated him. The building was shaped like a capsule, heavier on the bottom than on the top. Its outer skin was a fabric unfamiliar to him. There were also layers of windows wrapped around its cylindrical frame, the uppermost floor being outlined entirely in glass. *Good place for a telescope.* An opening in the cliff led to a heavy footbridge made of a kind of grey plasticky girder at the end of which an outdoor light marked the building's entrance.

An opening in the cliff? Ned did a mental double-take. If there was an opening, then maybe there was an entrance up here. He felt like a sitting duck on a mountain in the middle of a thunderstorm. So grabbing his all-weather jacket and a few necessities, he began a search. Far back from the edge was a large square platform surrounded by railings and signed-posted CLERY INTERNATIONAL LABORATORIES INC., NORTHERN PEAKS DIVISION – This Way >>>. 'This Way' was pointing downward to a set of stone stairs. *Clery, huh?*

The steps inside the mountain had seen better days. The passage was badly lit, especially in all this inky blackness. If he took the stairs slowly he reckoned he just might be able to make it without spilling out at the bottom. He had fallen over too many cliffs already to feel comfortable at that thought. It was a great relief when he finally stood on the footbridge outside an open threshold to a long white ultra-modern hallway. A sign over the door said "Welcome".

Do the rules mean that I can't go in? No, the door is open, the light is on, it says 'Welcome' ... What could be clearer?

A man in a white lab coat raced past the doorway calling out, "Come in, come in! Those doors stay open when we have a power cut. Don't want to get ourselves locked in do we? Just look around while I deal with the damage. We're a bit dim in here on the back-ups until I can get it fixed."

It was starting to rain and Ned was glad of any shelter, but this one was better than most. The first open door he came to along the hallway said: The Clery Museum. *That should be interesting. Here's where I'm sure to find the best examples of stuff from my present displayed as antiques in this future ... or something like that.*

The room was laid out with artefacts on sleek metal counters. High up the walls near the ceiling was a border of back-lit images, from molecules to galaxies. Ned examined the physical technology on a table just inside the door. There was a computer like his recent birthday gift in a line-up with several other models. They got less boxy and smaller in ascending order by year of invention. At the end of the table was a bucket of plain blue tennis-sized balls with a sign that said, "Tour guides ... Take one ... Swipe to begin ... Palms Only Please". Ned swiped. "Welcome to the Clery Museum," it said. "We recommend that you browse in a clockwise motion to best enjoy your experience."

On the wall to Ned's left a slide show began with images that were instantly captivating. The first slide read: "Lunar Bio-dome Project – Phase One, First Director, Dr. C. K. Arthurs". A bong triggered the ball. "At the beginning of the twentieth century, a scientist named Chester Kenneth Arthurs developed technology ..."

Wow! The moon project is shared with the world in the future. Ned watched the complete presentation feeling most delight at the familiar bits.

If he found this slide show interesting he was completely bowled over by the next one: "Lunar Bio-dome Project – Phase Two, First Director, Dr. O. M. Applegate." The speaker ball explained. "One hundred years after its inception, the lunar project expanded under the guidance of Oliver Michael Applegate, who discovered life under the moon's surface and found a means to communicate ..."

Good old Oliver, Ned thought with a chuckle, as he watched it through to the end.

"How are we doing in here?" asked the young man in the white lab coat who had just entered the room with an engaging smile and an extended hand.

"Interesting ... fascinating," said Ned.

"Isn't it just?" the man agreed. "Fancy seeing where the real stuff happens? Got the power fixed. We should be alright now. Let's grab a cup of something first while I give you the background. Tea? Coffee? Filtered water? Moon jelly?"

"Moon jelly?"

"Yeah, don't know what it's made from but it's completely 'more-ish'. Can't get enough of the stuff myself."

"Moon jelly, I guess."

"Are you Ned by the way?"

The question made Ned choke on his jelly. *How could this guy know my name?*

"It's just that we have you on our schedule to visit anytime now. Funny, there was no date mentioned, just that there would be a lightning strike first and a guy named Ned would pop in for a visit. That you ... Ned?"

"Ned. Yes, that's my name. I didn't have time to make an appointment."

"No matter, someone did. I'm supposed to give you the million dollar tour with a bit of background to the place."

Ned mentally called out to the Rhyll. *Did you do all this?*

"No Ned, although we know how it was done."

Curious and curiouser.

"Precisely."

The young man scooped the last of his jelly into this mouth. "Hi. The name's Tao Kai. I should have said that right off shouldn't I? Questions so far?"

Tao Kai was a small man, young for the job, older than Mercy Applegate had been, however. He had thick black hair combed straight down with one wide white streak overhanging his forehead. His golden-toned face was clean-shaven; his almond-shaped eyes were dark brown with rusty flecks. He wore a lab coat close-cut to his frame, collarless although not without pockets. Two large pockets were stuffed with interesting rubble – coloured bits of wire, a strange looking screwdriver, a rumpled handkerchief and a half-eaten sandwich. Under the coat he wore clean-cut black pants and matching shirt in a thin, wrinkle-free fabric.

"I guess my first question would be 'what is this place doing here?' I mean, we're up here on a seriously tall mountain away from civilization."

"Well I object to the observation about being uncivilized ... otherwise I take your meaning. We're up high to escape the pollution that an overpopulated world seems so good at producing. It's the only place where we can see the sky clearly enough anymore to use our super telescopes. But we think it's civilized up here ... getting more so all the time as people are settling here to escape the crowds. You know, a place to breathe deeply despite the thin air."

"This is an astronomy lab?"

"Oh yes, I thought you knew that. We're mostly about astronomy, though we've given over basement space to a small group of scientists studying geology and botany. They're trying to understand this part of the world better, while we're trying to discover more about space."

"I see ... am I right to think that the glass-sided upper floor I saw ...?"

Chapter Eleven

"Yup ... is set up for our super smart telescope: The E. C. Clery Telescope to be precise. Would you like to take a look? It's estimated to reach twenty-five billion light years into space!"

That's even bigger than the last one I looked through. E. C. Clery? I wonder who that was, or will be? Ned reflected.

Tao Kai led him along a series of hallways through doorways that opened automatically now that the central power had been restored. Ned was particularly interested in the series of telescopes developed by the Clery Corporation that were currently available for purchase. "We keep all the products we make in these self-cleaning rooms, just as well because all of us here are domestically-challenged."

"Do you live here also?"

"No we live in Cliff House, that residence you can see in the distance. We take eagles to work. They're just massive; they can carry at least two humans at a time."

"You fly eagles?" Ned's head was already fully charged with all the future technology but to add magic to the mix? He could barely cope.

"No we just get on their backs and hold tight; they do all the steering. Don't ever let an eagle think it's not in charge. We negotiated the deal through the empyreans when we first arrived."

"Empyreans?"

"A bit smaller than us, with these great feathery wings. You'll probably meet a few while you're here. Anyway the empyreans did the deal with the eagles – free rides between Cliff House and the Labs in exchange for a steady supply of the eagles' favourite meats. Eagles hate flying into the lower south to catch their own food anymore. They say it's just too dirty."

"You get about with eagle power? I wondered how you did it. I could never have guessed this!"

"Yea but we still use the public air shuttles to take us south when we have a few days off. Most of us have second homes back there; some of us have families."

Ned felt that his head just might explode any minute. He was full of questions, hardly knew where to begin. They had arrived at the uppermost level on a hover lift and Tao was approaching an enormous telescope, reachable from another self-rising platform.

Tao was working the gears to the Clery Telescope, making noises of frustration. "Can't get the super-scope part to work. This has never happened before." He jumped off the platform scurrying over to a locked compartment at floor height. He undid the latch, slid back the panel and shoved his head inside. "Nope." He lay on the floor holding his head sideways to try to see underneath. "Nope." He even got out the strange screwdriver from his pocket, turned it on to scan all the gubbins before his final conclusions ... "Nope."

"Nope?"

"Nope, I never learned how to repair it. Always knew the maintenance robots would take care of that, but they've already been this month. Must have been the lightning strike. This could be a problem ..."

Ned took a look at the inner workings himself. In fact it was surprisingly simple in structure, very neat. No mess of wires, no sloppy soldering. A few circuit boards and chips ... *Oh my!* Ned could barely contain his excitement. *I know what's wrong, but with the 'rules' I can't say.*

"Just so," agreed the Rhyll in his mind.

It's easy, it's just so easy ... Argh! It was mental torture for Ned to hold his peace. He was positively jumping up and down inside.

"I know what's wrong," a tiny voice said. A little girl stood beside them in front of the open panel.

"You do?" Tao said.

Really? thought Ned.

"Who are you?" Tao asked.

"I'm Annie," the little girl said. "I've seen that telescope before, seen it inside."

Annie was a pretty child with violet-blue eyes, a sweet freckled face and unruly auburn hair. She was wearing a yellow jersey nightgown under a light blue cardigan.

"Ah Annie, of course," said Tao. "You're the second one I was told to expect."

"You were?" Annie and Ned asked in unison.

"It's on the books. Annie, you say you know what is wrong with this telescope?"

"Yes I've seen one before. It's the solar opal. It's gone dull, needs replacing."

That's what I would have said if I had been allowed! screamed Ned internally.

***

"Why don't you wait for me over there at Empyrean Pavilion?" Tao suggested to Annie and Ned when their long tour was over. "Just follow the series of bridges to the cliff extensions. It's pretty obvious from there ... The huge light globes will guide you. I need to finish up my shift report. Then I can show you the sights ... maybe introduce you to the guys?"

"Sounds good," said Ned confidently.

"Sure," said Annie less confidently. As they stepped into the cool night air her teeth began to chatter. Ned remembered her thin night dress. "Take my coat. You'll freeze out here."

"You'll be c-c-cold," she protested.

"Oh, I have my locha... my long underwear, under my clothes."

Empyrean Pavilion. What a great name! What a great place! Walking along the cliff extensions was a bit unnerving, as it always was with no railings to keep an awkward guy from falling. It was primarily used by winged creatures, Ned supposed, who didn't need to worry about falling off anything.

Those 'winged creatures' made Ned's adrenaline soar. They were lochamours, without the fish tails and gills, but with wings!

He was certain of it. They had that same look about them, skin tones that complimented the hair, bright sparkling clothing, that soothing way of singing their words ... They were singing now and dancing to a four-piece band. The rhythms and harmonies of the music were like nothing Ned had ever heard. The notes went from very high to very low within seconds of each other, the tempo sped up and slowed down just as quickly. Ned found a spot back from the edge where he could sit, watch and listen. *I wish I could tell them about lochamours! I wish I could hear their stories ... I can't ... Right?*

"Right," said his inner Rhyll. In fact, Ned could just see his green crystalline friends on the other side of the pavilion glowing and thrumming to the beat. He knew the Rhyll would wait for him there. Right now he was more interested in watching Annie who had moved into step with the empyrean dancers. She laughed with delight as they showed her their moves, squealed when they twirled her into the air, hooted loudly as she played tag with an empyrean girl her own age, finally jumping on the back of an adult empyrean, as they all soared away into the night.

She'll be fine ... Won't she? "Should I go after her?"

"She'll be just fine." Tao said plunking himself down beside him with two more moon jellies. "Empyreans are the best! It's a great honour if you get asked to fly with one. Fancy riding an eagle?"

***

The way the wind ripped at his hair and clothing reminded Ned of that night with Bellflower on Nightmare. It was thrilling then, it was no less thrilling now. The eagle's body and huge feathers warmed him, making him feel safe. The ride was swift but smooth, as the eagle wafted around the narrow rock peaks where many more cliff homes were wedged. "Is it always this cold?" Ned shouted to Tao, as the eagle was dropping its talons to land on the roof of a brightly-lit complex.

"Nope, it's generally colder," Tao replied, sliding off the bird, "This is the middle of summer."

"I'd miss the beaches if I lived up here."

"Wait 'til you see what we've done about that."

***

"This is our version of the beach," Tao said as they entered an auditorium-sized space in the lower levels of Cliff House. "No sand sadly. The water is more like a deep pond than a pool. In fact it's two storeys' deep. It's all man-made of light materials to offset the weight of the water itself. They double-anchored this house, just in case."

In Ned's estimation this was the ultimate luxury. The scene seemed straight out of nature. Centrally spaced was an irregular-sized pond which stretched to within half a metre of the walls on all sides. The pond edge was surrounded by artificial trees, grass and rocks, with plenty of open space for sunbathers under the warm, unnatural lights. Three women and two men were stretched pond-side, drying off from a recent swim. "Would you like to take a plunge?" Tao asked, "We've got extra gear."

"Got my own on already," Ned replied, "'cuz you never know ..."

He hadn't swum this deep since his lochamour night. Nothing reminded him of that lake and those caves more than this place. Irregular rock formations had been sculpted here and there; Ned scooted around them in remembrance of his water-tag game years before. Underwater lights bounced off murals imbedded in rocky walls made of vividly-coloured shell fragments, with panels extending to the bottom far beneath. With Indigo assistance, Ned explored these in detail. They were telling stories, he was sure of it. Although some were vaguely familiar, still he could not quite figure out what they were saying.

After he had been submerged for ten minutes or so, he felt a hand grab his elbow pulling him upwards. It was Tao wearing a scuba tank looking very worried. Ned nodded and surfaced with him. "What the heck man!" Tao shouted, shivering.

"Where did you learn to swim like that?" asked one of the women of Cliff House, as they dried themselves in front a fake fireplace made of clear glass.

"Yea, you nearly gave me a heart attack," Tao muttered.

"Summers at Island Lake," Ned said, in partial response.

"Which is ..."

"South."

***

Ned was sitting on the cliff extension again close to the vacant pavilion not far from the Rhyll, after being dropped off by an eagle. It had been a great evening, full of surprises, very different from his former journeys. In fact despite all the confusing science, unfamiliar creatures and unconventional architecture, the evening had been most relaxing. No dramas, no near death encounters ... and he didn't want it to end.

"Hello ... again," said a familiar tiny voice – Annie.

"Hi Annie," he said kindly. "Nice evening?"

"The best!" she replied. "I think it must all be a dream though."

"It seems like that sometimes to me as well." Ned went over to pick up the Rhyll.

Before he had even touched it, Annie shouted at him angrily, "Hold it! That's my thingy."

"Thingy is it? Is that what it's called?"

"I don't know what it's called ... I found it."

"Ahhhh—ha." Ned looked down again at the Rhyll – at the Rhylls! There were two of them snuggled together. He squatted beside them in amazement. His own Rhyll companion was very familiar of course. Although the other was similar, he could distinguish the two by the differences in their caps and stems.

Ned stood looking at Annie while he checked with the Rhyll. *How much am I allowed to say?*

"Do you remember what the young lochamour lass told you?"

I'm unlikely to forget. Ned looked over, smiling kindly at Annie who was standing uncertainly some distance back. "Do you see that there are two 'thingies' here Annie?"

Annie made her way over, stood by his side, eyes wide. "Oh yes. How did that happen? How did any of it happen tonight?"

Ned remembered that feeling. "This thingy is with me; that one is with you."

"What is it anyway?" she asked, cradling hers in her arms.

"It's called a Rhyll ... and it has amazing powers," Ned explained in Aqua-Marie's own words, "It brought you here and it will take you home."

As Ned walked away he felt reluctant to leave the child near the pavilion, still wearing his oversized jacket, looking only slightly less confused. He was almost to the bridges when he stopped, turned around to look at her again, returning to sit down on the platform to think through a notion that had just occurred. Annie came over and sat by his side.

"How come you know about solar opals Annie?"

"I think my great-grandfather invented them ... o-or something."

"Really?"

"Yup, Edward Charles Clery."

"The same guy who invented the big telescope?"

"Yup. I recognized it right away."

"I see. So your name is ..."

"Annie Clery."

Ned had a feeling that he had been very stupid. Maybe he shouldn't ask. Maybe he should say nothing. But he just had to. His next words were chosen carefully.

"Isn't that strange Annie? Because my name is Clery too – Ned Clery."

"That's real funny. That was my great-grandfather's name!"

"You just said it was Edward Charles Clery."

"Yea, but everyone called him Ned."

Ned felt a bit dizzy at this detail. Edward Charles he was born, Ned he was called! What a ninny! With or without the Rhyll's permission he just had to know, "Do you remember your great-grandmother's name?

"Sure, I was named after her."

"So her name was Annie Clery?"

"No, my full name is Annie Maeve Clery. Her name was Maeve."

***

"Maeve?" asked Ned, as they lay back on the grass watching the August meteor shower pass overhead two weeks later.

"Yes Ned?"

"Would you say that you had an open mind?"

"What do you think?" she laughed, "I've been your friend all these years. That requires a very open mind don't you think?"

"Because I need you to have an open mind when you see what I have to show you. You will need to open it wider still when you hear what I have to say."

Chapter Twelve:
The Perfect Pot

The fire crackled pleasantly behind the ancient stone hearth as the old man stoked the coals. He had been sitting in that dusty old armchair for an hour or more letting the heat soothe his aching joints and spent muscles, content in his solitary reflections. These days he lived for the most part in memories, the active life much behind him now.

He needn't have been alone this evening of course. Malcolm, his carer and driver, had been with him all day, up to a short while ago. His cook had handed them an old-fashioned packed picnic before they had set out for the house that morning, plenty of nibbles to last the entire day and more. They had been packing what remained of his personal things into cases all day long, stacking them into one room to await their removal the next day. There was plenty of clutter to sort out for the trash which Malcolm would set out at the curb in the morning.

Of course he was leaving most of the furniture behind with the house. He had no use for it now and besides it wouldn't fit in with the modern decor in either the main house or any of the guest cottages on his estate. He couldn't imagine that his grandson would want much of it either when he moved into the old house with his young family as agreed, but he would let them decide what pieces to keep and what to give away.

There were those who scoffed at him for hanging onto his crumbling family home for this long, for leaving it vacant when he had no intention of living there again. But he had found it hard to let go and even harder to explain why – why he loved it so, and why he still visited it twice a year, had done so since he left it as a young man. His wife knew of course, had known almost from the beginning. She had understood. It was a secret that they held between them all of their lives. A secret that bonded them closer, if that were even possible.

But now she was gone...

He glanced down at his wife's engagement ring that he now wore on his little finger, a diamond that glowed unnaturally bright, a growing stone. How he missed his wife! Missed her every day. It seemed like only minutes that they had been allowed, although it had actually been more than eighty years! They had been to-gether for so long that there wasn't one thing in his life that didn't remind him of her, the children especially, and the grandchildren. And now the grandchildren had their young families too.

He would have given it all up in a heartbeat for just one mo-ment more of her. What did any of it matter anyway? She had been his greatest adventure, the one he never wanted to come back from. And for all his fame and the respect of his peers, he was still just an ordinary boy who had had the use of extraordi-nary magical tools.

Despite Malcolm's protests, he had dismissed him for the eve-ning, after the carer had placed fresh sheets, pillows and blankets on his parents' musty old bed. But as he sat comfortably rooted in Dad's favourite chair, he considered remaining up all night like he used to do all those years ago. So he just sat there half-dozing in the armchair, muttering to himself, "It's either tonight, or the full moon in April ..."

"Ned."

The old man stirred.

"Ned."

Is that you Rhyll? He wanted it to be more than anything, but he could not believe it would be true.

"We are here."

"Where have you been!" he shouted out peevishly.

"We have been here. You have been on an adventure of your own making."

"Maeve, yes. She's gone now ... did you know?"

"Regrettably ... a great loss ....   Shall we journey together again do you think?"

Thought you would never ask. I've got a great pot!

"We shall wait in the garden."

Ned pulled himself out of the chair standing still for a moment while his joints fell back into place. He made his way to the room where the packing cases had been stored and began rooting about. *I'm sure it was still here at the house. We kept it here, waiting for the next time ... there was no next time ... until now.*

Without any regard for the mess he was creating, he started ripping open the boxes, pulling out all their contents, undoing a complete day's work. The tape was so tough that his fingernails started to bleed with the effort. After two hours, and forty boxes, he had to admit defeat.

"Ned."

"I know, I know Rhyll, but I just have to find this pot. It's important."

He struggled upstairs to his third storey bedroom to search his childhood hiding places. In one he found the beat-up copy of <u>Robinson Crusoe</u> which gave him pause for a moment ... *Neville.* He dropped the book into his jacket pocket. Then he searched through old drawers, behind his narrow bedstead, under that loose floorboard. Nothing, no pot.

He went back down to the main floor and searched through Mom's kitchen cupboards, went all through the pantry. There were pots from the past, not *the* pot. He went down to the basement to Dad's workshop – a few rusty tools still, nothing more.

Next he put on his coat, boots and scarf and headed outside. The night was crisp as the first snow was falling like powdered sugar covering the sleepy garden beds under the full moon of

Chapter Twelve

December. The little snow that was beginning to cover the grass crunched under his boots, as he made his way slowly to the old greenhouse at the top of the garden, a long walk for him now. Several window panes were cracked; two had been boarded over completely. When he tried to open it, the door left its hinges and fell back, just barely missing him as it crashed onto the weedy lawn. His knees creaked as he pulled himself over the threshold. He had never noticed how high that step was before. Inside the single room was dusty and bare. Under the faint reflection of the moon he could just make out the tall plant shelves that had been so important in his youth. Now sadly no pots at all. He sat down to think, trying desperately to recall.

I don't think I took it to our new house. It could have made its way there of course without me knowing, I was that busy back then. If it isn't here I'm sunk I suppose.

He could picture that pot clearly in his head; could picture that moment when he received it. He and Maeve had been married a year. They had been broke at first, both being graduate students still and they lived here with his parents. With no money to speak of, they had decided to make their gifts for their first anniversary. He had cheated just a little with his, had commissioned a jeweller to put one of the solar opals into a plain silver setting on a thin silver chain. She had loved it; said it felt warm on her skin; said she would wear it forever.

When it came time for her gift to him, she had become embarrassed, hadn't wanted to give it. She said that next to his it was nothing, stupid even. He had insisted, tearing off the wrappings before she could pull it away. Inside was a wonky looking pot that she had made on a friend's pottery wheel. It was pure white ceramic clay with a clear glaze. It was meant to be rounded but it had gone a bit astray. While it was still wet she had imprinted it with her own fingertips in a ruffle all around the top. Inside she had placed a plain white card with the words, "For your next adventure – may I come too?"

This was better than my gift and you know it, old Ned muttered to her memory.

He walked back to the house glancing sideways at the Rhyll in his ruined old garden bed. It had been years since it had seen a vegetable. It was so overgrown in fact that it was hard to distinguish the edges.

Back in the house, he sat again in the chair, closing his eyes.

"Ned."

I am coming I promise Rhyll, just let me think about this. It always works when I close my eyes. He sat for a full half hour with his eyes shut, trying not to panic when that was precisely what he was tempted to do. Suddenly his eyes opened wide. *It must be there, that's the only place left.*

He made his way wearily down the side steps to the outer door again. By the light of a dim wall sconce he started opening trash bags, overturning them on the stairs until he came to it at last. Maeve's pot, made by Maeve's hands, with Maeve's fingerprints around the rim.

Returning to the living room, he mentally called out the Rhyll. *A few minutes more ... Will you wait?*

"We await."

He took the pitcher of water from the table beside Dad's chair and poured it on the fire's dying embers. Then he opened the briefcase at his feet and pulled out two small items, two envelopes, a single piece of paper, and a pen. The first item was a memory chip which he placed into one envelope. The next, the solar opal necklace that Maeve had worn all her life, he placed in the same envelope giving it a lick to seal them in. On the outside, he wrote "for Annie Clery – to be opened <u>by her alone</u> on her 15th Birthday – NOT BEFORE."

On the single sheet of paper he wrote, "Don't wait up." This he placed in the second envelope, sealing it with, "To my children and many other loved ones ..."

Chapter Twelve

He looked about the house through all those childhood rooms, turning off the lights as he went. Next he waded through the garbage at the side door and went into the garden again, his heart full of anticipation. He moved across the frozen lawn straight to the Rhyll in his garden, dropped to his knees, scratching at the frozen soil. *I don't have any good soil left in the greenhouse. This will have to do.*

"We have never needed the soil Ned. But it always seemed to please you and we did not object."

Right, always learning ... can you get in by yourself?

"Yes of course. You are old, we are not."

It took all his strength to get from his knees to an upright position and he was sweating by the time he got to the greenhouse once more. He placed the Rhyll in Maeve's pot on the rickety plant table while he struggled to pick up the fallen door. Though it took him a while, with a great deal of effort, at last the door jiggled into place held there by a wish and a prayer.

He grabbed for the pot as he slumped to the floor in utter exhaustion. From the window he could see the promise of a sun just starting to show under the horizon; the moon nearly washed from the sky. Still panting he loosened his scarf just enough to pull out the tiny leather pouch that he always wore about his neck, and taking out the Indigo, he placed it under his tongue. When his breathing had returned to normal he smiled down at the Rhyll. *Am I too late*?

"No Ned. We have your journey prepared."

But you know my heart?

"Of course."

And Rhyll ...

"Yes Ned."

This isn't our last adventure. You still owe me one.

"Just so."

***

There were rumours the next day, and for years to come, about this green glowing streak that shot up from the ground into the early morning sky from the edge of the old part of the village, vanishing from sight. Gossip also told of that old greenhouse in the Clery's back garden that had been there one day and gone the next.

***

As Annie Clery later recalled there was a full moon and a cloudless sky that night in the month of August in the tenth year of her life – that night, that exquisite moment, that delicious second when she first introduced herself to the Rhyll. Of course she didn't know at that time that it was a Rhyll, she learned that later. All she knew was there was a strange, mysterious ... alien-looking 'thingy' she would call it for now, growing at the base of her new tree-house that she and her parents had just finished that day in that gnarly old tree next to the bare patch where the old greenhouse had been. It only took the briefest of glimpses from a distance to launch her spirit of adventure. She didn't even know that she had a daring bone within her and she didn't even know what that meant yet. But once she saw what she saw from her third storey window, there it was – her adventurous spirit.

Acknowledgements

A special thanks to my early readers ...

Malynda Duern
Elizabeth Duern
Judy Duffin
Kelly Bentley
Brenda Worsnop

and to my first young reader ...

Isaac Coates

My sincere appreciation for the professional advice of ...

Paul McElhone
Jerome Martin
Chris M. Worsnop
Mark Leslie

...and for the inspiration of the iPad Artist Facebook Group

NANCY GUILD BENDALL writes and paints from her studio at the edge of a small village near Toronto Canada, looking all the while for fairies at the top of the garden.

nancyguildbendall.com

ISBN: 978-0-9939049-0-5